I0771723

Dean
&
Haley

W. Winters &
Amelia Wilde
Wall street journal & usa today bestselling authors

From USA Today best-selling authors
W Winters and Amelia Wilde

There was a girl in the corner.
She saw what they did to me and I saw what they did to her.
Except when the lights were off and when they put us in
confinement.
I was 16 and I don't know how old she was. We couldn't talk;
we couldn't even look at each other.
That would lead to punishment. I was punished a lot
because I had to see if she was there.
There were dozens of us and yet at night, it was only her
that helped me sleep in that nightmare of a boarding school.
They thought I was bad when they sent me there... little did
they know the monster they created.
I didn't know her name, but I knew who ran the school.
Years later and with blood on my hands, I got my revenge
planned years ago when I was only a child.
Then I found a name.
Her name.
If you thought they fucked me up, you should see what
happened to her.

My angel.

However You Want Me

Prologue

Dean

Tonight feels different.

Almost like that first time when I saw her across the room and knew she was innocent and worthy of so much more than this. We're so close to the end. I know it. I can feel it in the marrow of my bones.

The evening air is crisp and my breath forms a fog outside her bedroom window. Behind me is only the woods since she lives on the backroad. It's quiet apart from the sounds of the night. The sky darkens as I slip my hands into the jacket pockets and watch her undress.

Just for me.

I know she does it just for me. The way she arches her back to tease me. Exposing her slender neck so I can imagine kissing her right there, just beneath the shell of her ear. Her curves toy with me and my needs as her blouse becomes a puddle of silk at her feet. Bared for me with only a strip of cloth separating her cunt from my prying gaze.

The glow of the bedroom light dims when she flicks the light off.

I can imagine the creak of the bed as she climbs beneath the covers. I've heard it so many times before. My cock presses against the zipper of my jeans and I hold back a groan as I force myself to leave her sight.

The keys in my pocket jingle as I make my way around the side of the house to the backdoor.

It'll all be over with soon. There will be nothing standing between us. Not the nightmares of what once was. Not the pain that lingers and keeps a grip on the thread of sanity I have left.

HALEY

It's all in my head but I swear I can feel him.

The sheets chill my naked skin as my eyes adjust to the dark. The bed is empty but I stare at the lone pillow, wondering how long it may remain that way.

My gaze drops to where the pillowcase meets the sheet and I know the notebook is hidden beneath it. I can feel its secrets, its confessions... the vivid dreams I've scribbled away in the darkest of the nights.

Turning onto my back, I let out a heavy sigh and close my tired reddened eyes. The relief is immense.

But then I see him again.

I see it all play out and my throat tightens.

If I had never kissed him... none of this would have ever happened.

It was a kiss that changed everything over a decade ago.

A single moment where we thought we could escape. The sirens wail in my memory, the flashing lights force my heart to race as if it's all happening now. As if I'd just pulled the fire alarm. As if we're racing down the hall in the middle of the night, praying for the Devil to stay soundly asleep in the heat of chaos.

Tears leak from the corner of my eyes.

"Run away with me," he whispered and it's like I can feel his warm breath kissing my neck like it did that night.

I stared into his desperate eyes, full of pain from what we endured, and I could only beg him, "Kiss me first."

The water sprayed down around us, as he stared back at me, his chest rising and falling. We'd already made our choice. What was one more going to change?

"I don't even know your name," he murmured as others ran in a blur behind him.

"I know you though. I see you." I told him and I've never felt so honest in my life.

That's when the screams started.

Breaking up the moment... and yet.

A creak from the hall floorboards pulls me back from the memory. Grounding myself in this moment where it is all in the past. This is only trauma brought back by the recent events.

"It's gone. It's over," I whisper and I don't know who I'm trying to convince.

A second creak, louder and closer sends a wave of goosebumps down my body, chilling me to the bone. My heart seems to pound louder and harder with a spark of renewed fear. I call out, my voice hoarse, "Who's there?"

CHAPTER 1

DEAN

He walks the same. That heavy footed boot hitting the ground sends a chill down my spine. My back tenses against the brick wall as I force my eyes to stay open and watch him walk from his car to grab a pack of cigarettes. The gravel beneath his feet does nothing to remove the memory.

Left. Right. Left. I hear footsteps all over again. *His* footsteps. Just like it was yesterday. Like I'm in the cot, urine stench and all, listening to him come down in the middle of the night.

The moon is full so there's plenty of light and I don't mind that he can see me.

Unlike back then when I wished I could just disappear whenever I heard the thunk of his heavy gait.

A truck pulls into the parking lot of the bar just as I stand up straight and focus on my phone. There's nothing on the screen but pictures of her but I don't mind passersby in the night thinking I'm texting someone. Some drunk patron trying to find a ride, maybe.

My heart races and a flash of faces forces adrenaline to course through my veins. The screams are something that's so hard to silence. Nearly impossible.

I try to remember what she told me. I try to think only of her. It's all too much sometimes. The memories and the nightmares that linger.

His footsteps echo again and it helps to remind me this is something that has to be done. They can't get away with what they did. Then it happens.

His footsteps, one after the other, they're off.

My heart drops and my blood runs cold.

Punishment. That's a punishment.

As my gaze focuses on him, silence descends. With a cigarette hanging from his mouth, he lights the end of it and takes a puff. All the while walking to the side of the building where cigarette butts litter the gravel.

He's alone. Just as he is nearly every Tuesday night. And Wednesday and Thursday and nearly every fucking day of every fucking week.

Maybe that's how he deals with what he's done... he drinks his sins away.

My throat is tight as I swallow and keep my hands in my pockets, my left holding the basic utility knife, the pad of my thumb running circles around the metal.

He lifts his head back in greeting as I make my way to him.

It's nearly midnight, the bar is only open for a handful of regulars. I wonder if they'll even find his body tonight or if he'll lay in the puddle of ash and blood all night.

Maybe the animals will get to him. After all, he's close enough to the trash.

The corner of my lip picks up just slightly as I ask him, "Got a light?"

His head lowers as he looks down to his pocket.

I watch his hands and remember them on my shoulders, his fingers digging into my flesh in a bruising grip. 'Straighter!' he'd scream in my face and I swear I'd try. I can smell his breath. Cigarettes. 'Straighter you little shit' *Whack!*

I swallow as he looks back up at me and offers the lighter. He has to hold it out a second too long. "You going to take it?" he asks.

"Shit," I tell him. "Forgot my cigs."

He pushes off the brick wall, the prick is my height now. For a fraction of a second, I think he might recognize me, but he doesn't seem to.

"You trying to bum one?" he asks then adds, "*Bum.*"

As he takes a step forward, I remember the times we were

this close before. When I couldn't fight back.

"Do you remember me?" I ask and his brow creases as if he's trying to think of where he can place me. *How can he not remember?*

I don't mean to do it so quickly, I wanted to ask him so many haunting questions. The thoughts that keep me up at night... but I suppose they'll go unanswered.

I strike out with my left hand, blade to his throat, once then twice. With each jab I pull up, slicing the inner cords and making the most of every stab. Wide eyes stare back in shock and then I do it again. His hands reach up, first towards me, but quickly to defense. To try to block another blow. To try to keep the streaming blood from the gashes in his throat.

His knees give out and he falls to his back. Sputtering blood as he tries to scream out for help.

"Let me help you remember, Mr. Jay." I speak calmly as I lean over his body under the sole light that hangs down the alley. With one foot on either side of him, and the blood spilling from his neck and mouth, I lean closer to make sure he can hear me.

His eyes are full of terror and I think then, maybe he remembers.

"Welcome to hell," I hiss and stab again and again and again.

It's over in only minutes. All of it. Including the cleaning of the blade and slipping the jacket inside out after wiping off any evidence from my hands and face. I carry the bundle under my shoulder and the gravel crunches beneath my feet as I head back to my truck around the corner.

After I climb in and turn on the lights I look back to the bar. One person leaves and I watch the car go, none the wiser that there's a dead body only ten feet from the entrance, hidden only by trash bags.

I nearly leave before I cross his name off, but I remember. Taking the note from my back pocket. I see the one side first, her name and address and then turn it over. A list of names, seven of them, one already crossed off stares back at me. With the pen from the cup holder, I cross off Jay Danning. I'm surprised the mark is so clean compared to the first line I'd drawn through the name above. It's then I notice my heart pounds harder when I think of her than it does from what just happened.

Soon. It'll all be over soon.

CHAPTER 2

HALEY

10 YEARS AGO

Shame weighs on me, heavy and suffocating, but the fear cuts even deeper, slicing me to the bone.

The reality that weighs me down: I'm fifteen, and I've been arrested.

Arrested.

The word echoes in my head, driving the shame even deeper. Anxiety washes through me in waves.

Two men burst into my bedroom while I was sleeping and pulled me out of the bed. They handcuffed me while I stood there in my pajamas. I couldn't understand what they were saying. My screams didn't help. My pleas for them to stop. The terror was far too overwhelming.

Arrested? Me?

It was a bad dream. It had to be a bad dream. It couldn't be real.

I squeezed my eyes shut and tried to wake up.

But I didn't wake up.

Not even when they started to take me out of my bedroom. They weren't cops. Not real cops. They were kidnapping me.

I struggled, and my shoulder hit the poster that's been hanging on the back of the door since I was eleven. The actor's face tore in half, and the paper crumpled under one of the men's feet.

"Mom!" I knew she would come for me. I knew she'd stop these men from kidnapping me. That's what they had to be doing. Not arresting me, kidnapping me. "Mom, help!"

One of them slapped me. Fast. Unthinking. Like he done it a million times before.

Shock betrayed me, making my body still as they gathered me up making my fighting useless.

"Stop. Dad!"

I hadn't been getting along with my parents. They didn't like the friends I made at school. They didn't like the dark clothes I'd been experimenting with.

They didn't like how I'd stayed out a few times, unable to make myself leave.

But they wouldn't let this happen. They wouldn't! My parents were going to stumble out of their bedroom any second and save me.

I tried to shout it as we passed their bedroom door, but there was too much to say.

"Mom, please," I screamed instead. "Mom, they're taking me. Mom! Dad!"

But the door didn't open.

It stayed closed like they couldn't hear. I screamed until my throat was raw.

I stared at that door as they took me away, hoping, praying. *Open. Open. Open.*

It didn't open.

My stomach clenched with new terror. The men took me down the stairs and I couldn't see my parents' bedroom door anymore.

The fight went out of me when I got to the back of the car with the door slammed shut. That was like a nightmare, too. I knew they wouldn't let go, and that closed bedroom door broke something in me.

It's all I can think as the early morning sun starts to show and the car takes me away. It's silent. There's no way to fight anymore. I'm trapped.

Even if I got free, where would I run?

Outside, the neighborhood was silent. Curtains twitched in the window of the house next door.

I pulled against the men as hard as I could praying she would see and help me. The lady next door, Kathy, was always in everyone's business. She'd spotted me in my own backyard more than once and asked what I was up to.

Of all people, Kathy wasn't going to let kidnapping happen on our street.

Kathy's porch light stayed off.

Her front door stayed closed, just like my parents'.

I tried to call for her. She was my last hope. I knew she didn't like me, probably for the same reasons my parents had been so *disappointed*, but I still thought I meant something to them.

A hand clamped down over my mouth before I could scream her name.

"Don't make this worse," one of the men told me roughly. He sounded bored. Annoyed that I wasn't going along with this kidnapping. I couldn't remember what they'd said when they put the cuffs on. What charges? How could they take me to jail? *Why?*

The vehicle in my parents' driveway wasn't a police car. It was a white van with a door that creaked as the second man pulled it open.

The first shoved me inside and onto a worn seat with practically no cushion in it. A metal frame under the cloth dug into my ass.

There were more handcuffs, chaining me to the inside of the van.

"Where are you taking me?"

They climbed in the front seats, and the man who had told me not to make it worse started the engine.

"Which jail are you taking me to?" I don't even know how I'm able to speak with my heart rampaging as it does. I'm still fucking terrified.

They didn't answer.

If my parents wouldn't save me, and Kathy wouldn't, then maybe the police would listen.

I was naive enough to think they were taking me to jail.

We drove right past it and I thought I would cry but apparently the tears have all dried up.

Instead, we drive away from all the lights and onto back roads and highways. I can't keep track of where we're going. I don't know if they're making extra turns to confuse me, or if I'm just too shocked and tired and sick to remember them.

When the van rumbles to stop, it's still night. It might be very early in the morning. The sun isn't up yet. A single bare lightbulb shines down on a sign.

That sign scares me more than anything.

It's just a regular sign with the name of the school.

This can't be a school. The building doesn't look like a school, and schools don't kidnap students in the middle of the night.

But the sign could be in front of any school. It looks cheerful. There's a logo of an open book. All I know is something is very wrong and I have no way out.

The door of the van opens, and the men climb in to pull me out.

"Don't fight," he grits between his teeth.

I don't want to leave the van. My legs are numb from sitting on the hard seat and my wrists feel bruised from the cuffs, but the van seems safer than whatever this school is supposed to be.

"Where—" The men jostle me as they yank me out of the van and put me on my feet. The pain rips through my arm and it fucking hurts. They know how much bigger they are. They know they can push me around. I swallow the lump in my throat and try to keep the tears back as they surround me. Rocks dig in to my toes, scraping my skin as they hustle me across the driveway and into the school.

It doesn't smell like a school. Every school I've been inside smells pretty much the same—like lockers and the polish on the floor of the gym and the warmed-up food scent of the cafeteria.

This place reeks of decay, like a building that should've been torn down long ago. There isn't enough light to see much of it clearly, but there has to be mold—that wet, creeping smell like decomposing plants.

They take me to a room with a concrete floor and a drain in the middle. One man steps in and tears my pajamas off. I try to cover myself but I can't.

"Don't," I shout, over and over.

He leaves me with nothing. Naked in a room with two men and then goes to the right with determination while the other two stay on guard.

I'm not ready for the hose when it hits.

The second man turns on the spray full blast. It's freezing water, soaking my hair and my skin and taking my breath away.

I gasp and try to curl away like an animal. I can barely breathe. One shock after the next.

I'm an animal to them. A piece of meat. I shiver so hard I know there's another word for it—convulsion, I think, but the next frigid blast makes me forget.

I can only pray and try not to think about what's next. When the hose is off I cover what I can of myself and hope it's over.

"A towel, please," I beg. I can't even hug my arms around myself because of the cuffs.

A woman's voice answers. I didn't see her come into the room, but she's there in front of me, her lips pinched with disgust.

Tall. Her long, dark hair finished with a sweep of hair spray to give it volume. Her eyes are light blue and narrowed behind thin rimmed spectacles. She wears heels that click and echo in the room even though I can't see them, her wide legged black pants are so long they nearly touch the floor.

I want to plead with her to help me, but I can't make my voice work. My words are caught in my throat from the way she looks at me.

"No towel. You'll have to earn it," the woman tells me. There's no kindness in her eyes. Nothing but blank, dead emptiness. She doesn't see me as a person.

I'm not a person here.

I hug myself as best I can. My bones feel like they'll snap. Fear tightens around my lungs, letting me breathe only in sharp, shallow gasps.

She drags me to another room with the same rough concrete floor. My toes are numb, barely feeling the cold beneath them. She flips on a light—a flickering fluorescent light, too bright. On the side of the wall, there's a mirror. The woman's hand on my arm digs in hard enough to bruise. There are boys in the other room beyond the mirror. Her hand is at my wrist. She releases the cuffs from my wrists, and when I open my mouth, I open my mouth to scream for help.

I can't catch my breath. I can't scream. Even if I did, who would hear me?

When I raise my hand to my mouth to cover my sob, the woman yanks it back down and shoves me into the seat attached to a narrow desk.

The desk is the first thing I've seen that belongs in a school. It reminds me of the desks in my homeroom last year. I never thought of those desks as something normal.

This one isn't normal. It's the only desk in the room, and it faces the one-way mirror.

The woman grabs my face with her fingers and turns my head to look at her. Her thin fingers dig into my skin so deeply they hurt. I swear her nails will puncture my skin.

"You will not watch," she orders. "You will study your new rules."

Then she turns my head to face the window again.

There aren't any rules to study, except on the far wall of the room through the mirror. I struggle to read them. The woman stands behind me, close enough that I can feel her there but not close enough to touch me.

There's a man in the room with the boys. It's the middle of the night. Why are they up so early doing jumping jacks? It makes no sense. What's wrong? What's happening?

I hunch forward, shivering.

"Sit up straight," the woman barks, and pulls me up by my hair. I hold in my yelp and try to sit still. I try to do what she asks.

It's hard to sit up when I'm shivering so hard. The chair doesn't make it easier. The plastic is hard and cold, and I can't warm up. The room is cold, too.

The man in the room with the boys shouts something at them, and they start doing jumping jacks faster.

One of the boys looks through the window and meets my eyes.

"Faster," barks the man and the boy turns his head just slightly.

Can they see me?

Can *he* see me? I can see the boys, but I don't know who to believe. The boy's eyes stay on me, burning through the mirror. Maybe he *can* see.

I'm not supposed to look back at him, but the rules are written on the wall behind the boys. I can't help it. I don't want the woman to touch me again, so I keep facing forward and try to cover myself.

The woman paces behind me. Her footsteps are loud threatening in the room.

The man in the room with the boys looms over him, and he stops looking at me. He keeps doing jumping jacks, shoulders rising, arms, lifting and falling. An ugly bruise decorates his arm. My own arm throbs from where the men held me when they took me out of my bed.

That must be how they touch people here. How they handle kids like me. More of the boys have bruises, but I don't dare look too long. The words on the wall don't make sense, but I keep trying to read them.

I don't know how long it's been when one of the boys in the back breaks down crying.

"I'm tired," he says. "I'm fucking tired. I can't do this." He falls to his knees, begging, tears streaming down his face.

He's the only one showing any emotion. The other boys wear matching blank expressions as if they can't hear his cries.

The door in that room bursts open, and three men stream

in. They head for the crying boy, but not to help.

To restrain him.

They pin his arms behind his back and force him into a curled position that has to be excruciating.

I get to my feet and only realize it when the desk scrapes against the floor. None of the boys look at me.

"Sit down." The woman's hand digs into my shoulder.

"They're hurting him!" I scream as she shoves me down. Every inch of my body runs hot with fear and anger.

On the other side of the mirror, the boy's eyes flick towards me. One of the men has a taser.

He's going to use it on the boy who's being restrained.

It takes everything I have to stay upright and only watch. This isn't right. This just isn't right.

When the woman pushes on my shoulder again, I break away and run.

Neither of the doors is locked. I run into the room with the boys just as the guard leans over the restrained boy and tases him.

"Stop!" I shout over his screams, still cuffed, still naked. "You're killing him! Stop, stop!"

The boys move out of the way as I pushed through them, scrambling to do something. I grab the man's arm and try to pull him off, he turns the taser on me.

The electric pain crushes all the air out of my lungs. I crumple over the boy, my muscles seizing with more pain. It feels like it'll go on forever.

But then the door swings open and another man enters. I can't see, my vision blurry. But his footsteps are heavy. He walks a certain way. It's odd. Uneven.

The room falls silent.

I'm on the floor, my shoulder, trapped underneath me. I can barely focus my eyes to see the man when he crouches in front of me.

"You can call me Mr. Jay," he says. "What is rule number one?"

I can't answer. My teeth are locked together.

He sniffs, as if he's not surprised but I don't know the answer.

"You cannot look at another student," he tells me. That must've been one of the rules on the wall. "What did you do?"

I wrench my teeth apart.

"I don't know," I say. "I'm sorry. I'm sorry. Let me go home."

"There is no going home."

"But my parents—"

"Your parents know. They want this for you."

"They don't," I sob.

He shifts on his feet. "That's two more punishments. There is to be no mention of your parents and no backtalk."

He grabs my arm, fingers digging into the bruised spot where the woman held me, and pulls me to my feet. We're back in the dark hall in seconds. "Please," I beg. "Just let me go."

"You're adding up your strikes."

"What?" I ask confused as my feet barely manage to keep up with the pace he takes."Asking to leave is another strike."

A sound startles me. I crane my neck to see what it is.

The boys are doing jumping jacks. More jumping jacks— with two spots missing.

"That's another strike."

"What? I—" I looked at them. All I did was look.

Another room. Another concrete floor. A hard wooden desk. My heart is in my mouth.

The door closes with a hollow sound, and then leather slips through belt loops. He's taking off his belt. I turn to face the man, my arms over my chest

"What are you going to do to me?"

"The right thing." He swings the belt in his hand. "It's all in the pamphlet. Don't worry. Your mother knows."

CHAPTER 3

DEAN

PRESENT DAY

My dad's had the same recliner ever since I can remember. The worn brown leather, the soft creak that's gotten louder. The way it falls back when he drops into it. ...it's all familiar.

The chair is also broken, but Dad won't get a new one even though he sits in that chair every fucking day.

He's the kind of guy who worries about money and decisions like that. He pinches pennies and spends forever deciding which purchases to make. The house was always the most important. Had to pay the mortgage to keep the house.

The leather on his recliner is molded to his body and shiny in the spots where he always sits. There's a dent on the right arm where he rests his elbow when he holds his can of beer.

When he drops down into it, I let it go. He's never getting a new recliner and it's not like I can get him one. If I did, I don't know if he'd accept it. He's too damn proud.

My dad picks up the beer, balancing his elbow in that spot, and extends the footrest. The metal creaks. Probably needs some WD-40. Sometimes I think that chair will outlive me. My dad crosses his ankles, wiggling his toes and the white socks he buys in the big packs at the farm store.

I retake my seat in his living room watching whatever game is on TV. The sound is down too low to hear the announcers, and I don't' mind. Light slants through the blinds in the living room windows onto the same carpet that's always been here. No sense in replacing carpet when you can just have it cleaned—or rent the machine from the hardware store and clean it yourself. There's not much pile left after all these years. The carpet is worn pretty thin.

Still better than concrete.

I stretch on the ratty sofa and try not to think of so-called classrooms with concrete floors. The floors were what reminded me for so long after I came home. If I stretch enough, I can work the soreness out of my muscles and bring my mind back to Haley. I try not to think of her when the thoughts of back then are so raw. I try... but recently, I've been failing.

Easy to get lost thinking about her, especially when I think this game might be a rerun. I sort of remember what the score might be, but I don't really care. My dad isn't paying much attention either. It's just better to have something on then sit together with nowhere to look.

It's comfortable, I guess. House still smells the same as it always did—a mix of old wood and carpets cleaned too many times and wallpaper glue. Not much has changed around here. Same pictures on the walls. Same disintegrating coasters on the side tables. There's a round rug in front of the TV that used to be a mix of bright colors, but it's faded in the sun. That's the only sign that time has passed.

I'm the only other thing that's different. Although when I sit here, I can almost remember how I used to feel before. If I try hard enough, I can almost pretend none of it ever happened and I'm still the same.

Like none of it ever happened. But then I never would have met *her*.

That never works for long. My mind doesn't have to wander far to drag me back to the long nights and the screaming and crying and begging.

The punishments. There were always so many punishments. That shit never ended. None of us could ever do anything right.

It was designed that way. Tough love is what he called it when my father let them take me. I glance back at him and take a sip. He didn't know.

Sit up straighter. Don't look at them, look at me. What rule did you break? You broke it again. Straighter. You need to learn. You're here to learn. Your parents want you to learn. That's why they sent you here. So you'd learn. You're not that fucking dumb. Act right! You're such a fucking failure. You're never going back at this rate. They'll keep you here. Better for you here than out there where you're always hurting people. Why do you hurt them? You hate them, don't you? Don't you?

The screams echo in my head.

If you hear that kind of thing often enough, it starts to sound true. My arms would burn from lifting them up and up and up while we did jumping jacks until your body couldn't take any more. My feet hurt. Once I had a swollen ankle from when one of the teachers tackled me—damn thing was probably sprained—but I still had to do jumping jacks. Ankle's never been the same since. The pain never really went away.

Maybe it did, but I still feel it.

Haley. I should think about Haley. I'll never forget the rest of that shit, but I can choose to concentrate on Haley.

My memory of her is like my phone. Hundreds of images locked away even though I know they're there.

Sometimes she pauses, and something about the way she goes still makes me think she can feel me watching.

I like the thought of her feeling my eyes on her. It's like she saw me.

No one else really did. They looked right through me.

When her bedroom light is on, it's like a one-way mirror. She can't see me watching her, but I can see her. The curve of her neck. The way the fabric slides off her body when she takes her shirt off, smooth and deliberate. How she stretches her arms over her head, so beautiful, so perfect.

And then, when the light goes off, I know she's crawling into bed and the soft sheets are touching even softer skin and she's warming up the blankets with her body.

Maybe she still thinks about me watching when we weren't supposed to. She was the one rule I broke. One more reason I was convinced I'd die in that place. Maybe she touches herself, thinking about me watching. Maybe it turns her on to know I'm out there in the dark on the other side of the glass, all these years later.

My dad sighs and I'm snapped out of my thoughts. He picks up his can of beer from the side table, drinks, and sets it back down.

I forgot my own beer. The condensation from the can has soaked into the ragged coaster below it. I pick it up and take a swig and pretend I wasn't thinking about her ... and that place. The fan on the ceiling spins. It seems a little louder for a second, then gets quiet again.

The game switches to a commercial. It's definitely a rerun. We've probably sat here watching it before.

Out of the corner of my eye, I see my dad glance at me.

"You seem out of it," he says, tone gruff and casual.

I shuffle on the sofa and raise my eyebrows at him.

"Do I?" I question and play it off.

My dad shrugs, then turns to the TV again. His gaze is unfocused, more lost in thought than in the game. Or I guess the commercial for some weight-loss pill.

"You weren't here last night. Thought you were staying over." He talks without looking at me. His tone nonchalant but I know him too well.

"I was." The commercial changes. "Went to bed early."

"Oh. Guess I didn't hear you." My dad picks up his beer again, but sets it back down without drinking.

Adrenaline rushes through me but I stay still. *Don't ask questions Dad.*

Thoughts of last night try to trickle in and instead I focus on anything else. The living room is warm from the sun. It was never warm at that place, no matter how bright it was.

It was never warm until the summer came, and then it was too hot. The teachers had personal air-conditioning units and box fans that stayed on them, but we didn't have anything. During those few summer months it was like being baked alive in an oven. The concrete floors held all the heat in.

The teachers believed in keeping it cold until they believed in burning us to death. Never a middle ground. We had to earn comfort. It was a privilege.

I guess you could say I don't have a middle ground, either.

I go between memories of screaming and torture and wanting to die to memories of Haley through a window.

It's going to be over soon. All the shit that happened in the past is going to be taken care of. It'll be dead and buried, and then these thoughts can go away.

"You alright?" my dad asks quietly. I can feel him watching me.

"Yeah." I don't take my eyes off the TV. "Fine."

He doesn't say anything for a minute. There's a weight in the air, like he's getting ready to break some bad news. Don't know what bad news he thinks he has to tell me. I pretend I don't feel it and keep looking at the TV.

"I know," he starts, then waves his hand at the TV. It's just the game on the screen. "I heard the news."

"What news?" My jaw tenses and I wish he'd stop. We don't have to say anything.

"About the principal." He drops his hand into his lap and looks me in the eye. "Your principal from that... fucking nightmare." My dad's voice cracks.

I look back at him, my expression blank. That's a habit that came with me from that place, I'll probably never get rid of it. It's not smart to let anything show. My default is no expression at all. They taught me that.

My dad's jaw works, the look in his eyes changing. He doesn't like it when I look at him like this. He's said so before. But he won't like it any better if I try to change my face.

I won't, anyway. I can't.

"He's dead."

He's dead. The words land on the worn-out carpet like dust. My heart ticks up a little faster. It doesn't stay that way. My dad's not telling me anything I don't already know. Memories of that man's face come up like they happened yesterday, but I push them back down. He had the kind of face you could see anywhere, on any guy you passed on the street. That's the kind of face you can't get away from, even if you forget what he looks like.

I haven't forgotten any of it.

My dad hasn't looked away from me. He's waiting for an answer, some kind of response. The air between us is tense. He wants something out of this but I don't know what. He probably wants me to be the same kid I was before he sent me to that place. He's said it before. How much he regrets it.

"Mr. Jay?" he nudges the suggestion. "The principal of that boarding school you went to?" He tries to get me to remember or acknowledge anything.

I bury more memories of that asshole and the screaming and punishments and sitting up straight. The fact that he's dead has nothing to do with me.

I bury more memories of the building, and how, when I finally left, I didn't think the outside world was real. I spent years waiting to be taken back and put in those same rooms and left there for the rest of my life.

"He wasn't my principal," I say finally. I want him to drop this. I know he can tell. "It wasn't a real school Dad, remember?" I tell him flatly, easily. Like I'm unbothered.

He nods and opens his mouth like he might say more, but he doesn't.

We turn back to the game. I watch dust motes hover in the air and look through the doorway to the kitchen. The same old microwave, plastic all yellow with age, still sits on the counter. The damn thing looks like hell, but it hasn't died yet. It just keeps living and living, heating up food with a crackling sound and a little rattle where the glass plate isn't quite even. My dad doesn't care about that. He won't buy another one until this microwave burns out and all the wiring melts together.

"Dean." His voice is thick. The emotion he's trying to control makes me want to get up and leave, but I don't.

"Yeah?"

There's another long silence. Emotion fills the room, but it's outside of me. It doesn't make any difference what my dad feels. There's a twinge, I guess, somewhere deep down, but that's just as likely to turn into anger.

Sometimes, when I look in the mirror, I still expect to see myself at sixteen. I still expect to see him how he was, not this older, grayer version. Some of those years feel like they never went by at all and I hate looking at the evidence that they did.

"Look at me," he commands and I do.

My dad's face falls, his eyes shining.

"It has to be—" His voice is even thicker with sorrow. It's impossible to ignore now. "You know, I'm sorry." He clears his throat. It's always easier for him to sound angry rather than sad. That's fine with me. I don't need weepy apologies. "I'm sorry, Dean. I didn't know."

"You already told me that," I say confidently, offering him solace. It's true. He has told me that. He's told me that while he's crying and yelling and whispering. He was a wreck when he found out what they did. They closed down the school although no one was ever charged. Everyone got away with what they did.

He clears his throat again. Sounds like it hurts.

Part of me softens. Enough that I can make my eyes soften, too. "Dad."

He meets my eyes. I can tell he's trying to keep a straight face. I can also tell he wants me to bail him out of all the guilt. I don't want to see him like this, so I will.

"There's no way you could have known."

The breath goes out of him like he's never heard me say this before. He has. I tell him the same thing every time this comes up. He lives with the pain like I do. It's just different.

"Does it bring up... anything?" My dad tries. "Hearing that news."

There's nothing to bring up. The feelings are always there. The memories too. I bury the screams deep inside—the feel of the rough concrete floor, the knowledge that I'd never get out, that I'd die in that place, and they'd bury my body in an unmarked grave in the yard. I knew it was hopeless. I knew nothing would ever change. I buried those feelings too. It's not the news that makes them come back. They're always with me.

I make a sound and shrug. My dad can take it to mean whatever he wants.

"Did you tell your therapist?" he asks, sounding even more gruff. "Are you still going?"

I don't want to talk about any of this with my dad.

"They just gave me meds and they're working," I tell him. "Let it be, Dad. I'm alright."

He nods, then takes another drink of his beer. I can tell the can's empty from the hollow sound. He rests it on his thigh, tapping it a few times like that might make it fill itself up again. In a few minutes, he'll get up and get another can from the fridge. I hope he's lost interest in this conversation by then. If he hasn't, I'll think of some excuse and head out.

My dad shifts in his chair again. Guess he hasn't lost interest.

"What's your girlfriend say about it?" He sounds fake when he tries to be casual. "What's her name again?"

He glances at me, smiling, trying to get the two of us to be buddies. I prefer this. In a lot of ways it's a second chance.

I smile back at him. "Which one?" I say it like it's a joke.

The fond expression on his face is real. So is the laugh he lets out.

"You're a smart-ass, Dean," he says, and goes back to watching the game. "Love you kid. If you ever need to talk, you know I'm here." He says and then that old chair creaks as he gets up.

"I know Dad," I tell him and turn back to the TV, trying to forget like I do far too fucking often.

Chapter 4

Dean

10 Years Ago

We're never alone in this school. Should I even call it a school? It's a hellhole. Hell on earth. The worst place imaginable for the worst people imaginable. Like me... but they're worse.

I always thought that was supposed to be prison, before this. I knew people went to prison. I knew they got arrested and thrown behind bars and treated like shit.

But it's not really about laws or breaking rules in this place. It's not about being such a bad kid that our parents gave up on us.

It's not about anything but sick fucks getting off on ruining our lives.

So we're never alone. There are always eyes on us, even in the bathroom. No doors on the stalls. We can't be trusted.

The bathroom has a concrete floor like most of the other rooms I spend time in here. There's a drain in the middle of the floor. The concrete is almost always wet. They must have to spray it down a few times a day. More if they're going to beat the shit out of somebody in here, and they usually do.

It has tiled walls and a mirror made out of metal and a rusted metal sink. When the mirror was new, maybe I could've seen myself in it, but now it's just a metal plate with so many scratches and claw marks that there's nothing but a shadow reflected back.

The bathroom has one stall and one urinal along the other wall. No door.

I go to the urinal. The staff member who escorted me here leans in the doorway, looking annoyed.

I bite back a sarcastic *sorry*. Sometimes I say things like that just to remind myself that I'm alive, but until today, I wanted to be dead.

I don't want to think about that bastard in the door anyway.

I want to think about the girl.

Most times when I come in here, I like to think about the window. There's one window on the far wall. It's a narrow rectangle of foggy glass, so I can't see out. It lets a little light in, though.

Most times when I come in here, I let myself look at it just once. They don't like when I look out the window. They probably think I'm planning some escape attempt. But I just want to see something different.

Sometimes I do, but mostly I imagine scrambling up the wall and somehow bracing myself so I can punch the window out.

I think about how it would feel for that glass to break under my hands. Probably terrible, since it's probably thick, but when it finally broke—damn, that would be victory. It wouldn't matter if I cut myself or broke my fingers. I want to break this place as much as it's broken me. I want to rip a part of it off and make it bleed until it chokes out its last breath and dies in front of me where I can see.

That's just a daydream. I'll never have a chance to break the window. Even if I could climb that high and keep myself up there, I wouldn't have time. I'm strong enough to make it to the ledge, but like I said, we're never alone. The man standing in the door could reach me before I threw the first punch, and he wouldn't stop at pulling me down to the floor. He'd get a few punches in, too. I'd end up restrained at best and tortured by myself for who knows how long.

And then drugged up again. They force pills down the throats of the ones who fight back. They keep us weak.

I'm not thinking about that when I unzip the black slacks they gave me. I'm not even thinking about how that sick fuck is watching, or how they pretend it's for our own good. I'm used to the fact that we're never alone by now. I'm used to the smell of bleach and piss. I'm used to thinking that it smells like a prison and calling this a school is somebody's idea of a joke.

I'm not used to thinking about a girl.

I haven't stopped thinking about her since I saw her through the one-way mirror earlier in the night.

It's obviously not a one-way mirror. There's no sense arguing the point, though, because the people who run this place will just beat it out of us. There's no convincing them because they know they're lying. It's enough that I know I can see through that damn window.

It's a punishment if we do it. The lying. They scream in our face and the spit and smell of rancid coffee is enough to make me vomit. *Liar! Fucking liar!* They scream until my chest vibrates. Even if we're telling the truth.

But they can lie to us. They can say we can't see through it and we have to agree.

I was so surprised when I saw her sitting there. Her eyes were so wide and scared and sad, and she was still wet. Her hair all around her shoulders, wet and curling. She was shivering and cold, trying to warm herself up without moving. I didn't expect anyone to be brought in and I wasn't waiting for it.

I shouldn't have looked but I remember that day. I don't remember how long ago, it's been months since I was brought here at this point. Looking though... I shouldn't have looked.

That was just an excuse for more punishment, and my own mistake. I knew looking at her would earn me some strikes, and I knew saying anything about her would earn me more.

I was hoping she was okay though. If she just stays quiet and listens. She doesn't look like she could take what they do to people here.

I still can't stop thinking about her and the look on her face. I already know better than to make a face like that, but this girl—this beautiful girl—she's never seen anything like this before. She doesn't know what this hell is. She has no idea.

By now, she's not as innocent as she was when she first got here. They take that from you in the first hour. But she still has no idea how bad it can get. She might even think there's a chance of getting out.

I flush the toilet, pull up my pants, and wander over to the sink. The staff member at the door sighs and rolls his eyes. If I take too long at the sink, he'll drag me away by the arm.

I count in my head. Twenty seconds is all you're allowed. I'm going to wash my hands every chance they give me. It's one of the only things I can do to stay human, even though by this point there's not much humanity left.

Like when we had to keep going... although we knew what was happening to her.

During that hour, I didn't imagine the sounds I heard coming from the office down the hall—the crack of a belt, and anguished cries. I'll hear those cries for the rest of my life.

There's no doubt in my mind.

It was that girl. That was her voice. She was still human, too. That was her problem.

We're not allowed to be human here. Our parents send us here to become well-trained animals.

My thoughts fly back to her trying to help. Trying to save someone she doesn't know. Hell we're not even allowed to know each other's names. Maybe from outside of here... the thought hits me.

Did she know him? Is that why she did something so reckless?

He didn't seem to know her.

Either way, he'll spend tonight being tortured in a room alone to teach him a lesson.

What lesson?

Don't know. I don't think there's any lesson to be learned at all. They just want to break us so they can send us back to our parents as shells of ourselves. Shells are easier to deal with than a full person, I guess. It's easier to control a person who doesn't have any interest in living.

I don't want to live either. I would rather die than be here.

But that girl's eyes—

The way she still cared. I don't want them to take that away from her.

Her eyes make me want to stay alive. They remind me that there is a world out there. A world where people like that girl can come from. She's in hell with the rest of us now.

I've lost track of how many days I've been here. I only know that every time I fuck up, I'm staying for longer. That's what they always say. I'm adding punishments. I'm adding strikes. I'm adding more days and weeks and months. The only way out is to prove that I've learned. I've given that a try before. We all have. It never seems to work.

Some of the guys leave eventually. When they behave so well they're allowed to talk to their parents. Maybe their parents come to their senses. Maybe they finally manage to convince their parents of what's happening here.

I don't know. It's against the rules to tell our parents anything about this place when we are granted the privilege of calling them. When I first got here, I was so mad that I didn't talk to him even when I was finally allowed. That was months after they dragged me through the front doors.

I figured if he'd sent me to this place, he'd never believe me about what it was like. I still don't think he'll ever try to get me out of here. He probably forgot all about me. It's been so long that he has to figure I'm a lost cause.

I finish washing my hands and shake them dry. There's no paper towel in here. No hand dryer, either. There used to be a hand dryer at one point, but all that's left of it is a rectangular dent in the wall where it used to be. Somebody ripped it off the wall before I got here.

I wonder what that was like. I wonder how much they paid for it. More than it was worth. Nothing in this place is worth anything.

"Finally," the staff member grunts. It's not like I took extra time at the urinal. I ignore him. I keep my back straight and shoulders up like they tell us. I walk on the barely seen painted line on the floor. It's the only line we're allowed to walk on. "Come on."

I follow him back down the hall to the room where we sleep—rows of beds, too close together, eight of us in a room. My bed is on the far side of the room. There are no windows in this cell. Thought it was illegal to put this many people in a room without any windows. Just more proof we're not people at all.

They tell us enough. We act like animals. So we're treated like animals. We did this to ourselves.

I lie back down in my bed, the staff member breathing down my neck until I'm flat on my back. Laying perfectly straight like we're supposed to do. Palms up.

He stalks away, and I close my eyes. The bed is hell, too. A thin mattress with springs poking into me. I only have a sheet on top of the mattress. I haven't earned a blanket and probably never will. No pillow, either. I had one of those for about a week once. I can't remember how long ago that was. I can't remember what I did to lose it either.

So I lay my head on the wrinkled sheet over the squeaky plastic mattress cover and zone out. There are always people watching us—footsteps moving past the door, light shining in. I keep seeing flashlights shining in.

I let that stuff fade out. Best thing to do is keep my eyes shut and try to rest at least a little so I can get through another day.

So I have a chance of seeing that girl again. That's what I want to wake up for tomorrow. That girl and her eyes. To know she's still there. That bit of her that's goodness in this fucked up place.

I roll onto my side and keep thinking about her.

I'm almost asleep when somebody near the door screams.

Damn. It'll be twice as hard to fall asleep again now. I open my eyes, but I don't move the rest of my body. I stay still and in place knowing what's next.

Heavy footsteps come down the hall. Mr. Jay stomps into the dorm, his shadow huge in the doorway.

He leans over the bed and punches the kid in the face.

The kid gasps and lets out a strangled sob. Mr. Jay punches him again. The kid finally catches on and stops making noise. Nobody else moves. They're all still on their sheets or, if they're lucky, under their blankets.

"Out of the damn bed," Mr. Jay says to the kid. He's curled up on a bare mattress, his arms over his head. "Up." He's sobbing now. Why did he scream?

Was it in his sleep?

My throat goes tight and my eyes prick. I stay still knowing how many men are out there. Knowing if he just listens, they'll stop.

The boy at the end of the row gets out of bed. His hands go to his face. If he didn't have a broken nose before, he does now.

"Walk," Mr. Jay says. The kid looks like he can barely stay on his feet, but that doesn't matter to people like Mr. Jay.

They go out into the hall. The kid doesn't come back that night.

CHAPTER 5

HALEY

PRESENT DAY

It's almost dark when I walk up the sidewalk in front of Aden's house. It should probably be lighter out, but clouds rolled in this afternoon. It's spitting rain. Not enough to be satisfying, but enough that the droplets are starting to cling to my hair. I'm glad to step under the small roof covering his front porch and shake off the bit of rain.

There's no light on above the door, making it look like no one's home. I know better than that. The house always looks like no one's home. The grass is always cut, but the front lawn isn't landscaped. One of the previous owners planted a rose bush at the front of the house. It's still there, but it's not the kind of rosebush that someone looks after. There's a difference between the plants people tolerate and the plants people love.

I ignore the darkness on the porch and knock.

No one answers. There's no sound from inside, and no lights coming on.

My heartbeat slows a touch and anxiety seeps in. I shake it off. Everything's okay. I'm just shaken is all. Which is why I need Aden.

I knock again. Firmer this time. My knuckles turn white and the thinned skin over them actually hurts with each hard knock.

This time, there's quiet movement on the other side of the door. I know to listen for it, and that's the only reason I can hear. The footsteps don't sound like footsteps. If it was any windier, I wouldn't be able to hear them at all. They're whispers over the floor. The wood gives, but doesn't creak.

My heart beats faster as he approaches. I run a hand through my hair and take a deep breath.

I can feel him there on the other side of the door. I don't knock again, although I want to—just a soft sound to let him know that I know he's there.

I keep my hands at my sides.

The lock on the other side of the door disengages with a quiet scrape. The knob turns. Finally, the door opens to reveal Aden. He's dressed in jeans and a dark T-shirt, his feet bare and his eyes dark, like he hasn't slept. He only opens the door wide enough for me to see his face and keep it defensively in front of him.

I know what I'm looking for. I see the small signs of relief in his face. The twitch at his cheek. A softness around his eyes. Those eyes search my face. Aden exhales.

His lips part as if he might speak, but he gives a tiny shake of his head and closes them again.

I lean toward the door—toward him—but I don't press against it.

"I saw the news." I keep my voice soft and soothing and even, putting as much understanding and compassion into the words as I can. "Are you alright?"

His eyes dart to the left, and he swallows thickly. That muscle in his cheek twitches again.

"No." His eyes come back to mine, more alive than they were, almost burning with emotion. "I'm not."

We look at each other, a palpable current in the air. The breeze picks up, blowing between us, ruffling my hair. I wonder if he can smell my shampoo when the wind blows like that. I can smell him—a clean, spicy scent, his body wash warmed up.

For a few seconds, all I can see is his face—the sharp jawline, his hair mussed like he's been grabbing it. "I'm not either," I admit to him.

Aden narrows his eyes.

I don't know what he sees when he looks at me like this. I

wish I could look into his mind. But I'm here, in my body, my pulse fluttering and warmth spreading over my torso as our eyes stay on each other.

I lift my hand up slowly and place my palm on the door—not pushing, just suggesting.

Aden pauses, letting out a deeper breath.

Then he opens the door wider, inviting me in.

I step inside, into the warmer air of Aden's narrow entryway. One of the floorboards creaks under my feet. Aden backs up a little more, giving me the space to come fully inside, then reaches behind me to shut the door. It smells more like him in this house. The fresh air from outside mingles with us in the entryway.

I look up into Aden's eyes. "Are you okay?" He's not alright, but there are levels to that sort of thing. I change my question to a statement, "You're going to be okay, everything will be," I make a promise to him I can't keep.

A low growl escapes his throat. His eyes, dark in the dim light, get even darker. I was wrong before. There is one light on in his house—a small lamp inside the den. The light just makes it into the hallway to cast shadows on his face. My heart beats faster.

"I need you." Aden's voice is tight and rough. "Now."

"I know. I need you—"

Before I can finish speaking, one of his hands flies to my throat. He buries the other hand in my hair, clenching his fingers tight.

This. This is what I need.

"On your knees," he orders and between my thighs instantly heats.

I let him brace me down, helping things along by sinking to my knees.

"Good girl." Aden's eyes move over me.

"Please," I whisper. I let them come, sinking into the sensation of his hand in my hair, pulling on the edge of too hard, and the harsh tone of his voice.

He angles my face up and stares into my eyes.

"Just like that." Aden keeps his hand in my hair and uses the other to unzip his pants. He pulls out his cock, which is already hard and heavy and leaking at the tip. He wraps his fist around it and strokes, letting out short breaths as he watches my face. I keep my lips parted and wait.

"This is what you need me for," he says, almost to himself.

His hand flexes in my hair, he doesn't let go. He steps closer and drags the head of his cock over my lips. I let out a soft moan.

"You like it, don't you? Getting put on your knees."

I stick my tongue out and lick up some of his pre-come. Aden swirls the head on my tongue with a groan. My heart batters in my chest. Loving how he takes control.

"Fuck. You feel so damn good." He grinds into my tongue harder, the movement making a slippery, wet sound, then pulls back with a frustrated sound. "Fuck."

With my hands on his thighs, I hollow my cheeks and suck. I pull back letting his cock make a pop sound and leave my mouth open so he can throat fuck me.

He thrusts in slower, and I gag again. He groans, louder, and my body gets hotter. There's nothing like hearing those sounds from a man. There's nothing like hearing them from Aden.

With a needy grunt, he rolls his hips and begins fucking my throat with steady thrusts. All the while I can feel myself getting hotter and wetter. Ready for what he does next.

I make a noise around his cock. He groans again, his pleasure vibrating in my mouth. He likes when I do that—likes it a lot—so I hum some more like there's more I want to tell him. Aden grunts, his thrusts getting slower. His cock fills up my mouth, and my throat, pushing deeper and deeper one hand still in my hair.

"Fuck." When he speaks, his tone is softer. Almost with reverence.

I moan around his cock, encouraging him.

On his next thrust, I swallow him deep, then keep him where he is so I can lick his shaft and suck. More salty pre-come coats my tongue. Tears run down my cheeks from how hard I'm working to suck him off and from the head of his cock meeting the back of my throat over and over again.

The longer I stay on my knees, the needier I feel until I'm practically squirming. I want more, and Aden is always ready to give me more. He knows I need this.

I need him to fuck me.

He pulls out, and I gasp in a breath of air, then a second one. My chest heaving and every nerve ending on my body lit aflame with need.

"I'm sorry," I say. The words tumbled from my lips. Aden reacts to them as if I'd taken his cock back in my mouth.

"Shh—" He trails off, unable to keep up this part of the conversation.

Aden pulls me to my feet, his mouth, capturing mine. He kisses me fast and deep and frantic, his grip at my neck and his thumb at my throat. With another growl he stops, kissing me. His hands work at my pants. Aden strips them down and shoves them off along with my panties. He rips them away like they're a nuisance and I should've come here naked, exposed to him from the very beginning.

He bunches up the clothes and tosses them against the wall. Aiden's eyes roam over my face and my half-naked body. His lips glisten, nearly swollen, from our kiss, his eyes dark.

I feel everything all over again. That one moment. The one that changed everything.

Aden reaches for the hem of my top like he wants to tear that off, too, but instead his hands go around my waist and he lifts me off my feet, shoving my back against the wall. I curl my legs around his hips, feeling his length, hot and throbbing, surrounded by the rough denim of his jeans.

Aden drags his mouth over my neck, thrusting against me, the velvet skin over his erection sliding through my folds. *Fuck!* He curses in my ear, and I sling my arms around his shoulders and hang on tight. I wouldn't fall even if I let go. The pressure of his body would keep me against the wall. I dig my nails in anyway. Aden hisses at the feeling. His mouth meets mine again in a savage kiss. His body works against mine, and I rock my hips into him. I'll take any contact I can get. My body is already warm with pleasure and sparking with a kind of filthy need. All I can do is chase what he's offering.

Aden's meet the side of my neck. He doesn't bite hard, but his tongue laps at the skin.

"You need this don't you," he says, his cock nudging between my legs. He thrusts inside with one smooth stroke, letting out a deep groan. "You can't get enough of me."

"I can't," I agree and throw my head back against the wall. He's filling me in exactly the way I need him to. I didn't know who I was until he was inside me. "I can't."

"What would you do for this?" he demands, his mouth meeting mine and sloppy kisses. "Would you stay here and let me use you? Would you stay as long as I want you to? Would you stay here and never leave?"

"Yes," I answer, breathless. "I would do that. I need this. I need—"

Aden changes his angle so our hips are pressed together. There. That's the contact I needed. Every thrust hitting my clit and his cock buried deep inside of me. Aden gives me a longing look. One I know he denies but one I can feel deep in my soul. I feel it in the way he touches me—his hands tight and then gentle. He shoves his hand under my shirt and teases one of my nipples with his fingertip. He grinds into me harder, his breath coming faster.

"You'll come from this," he orders. "You could come just from me fucking you against the wall. You're going to come on my dick, just from this. So fucking beautiful coming on my cock."

"Yes!" I let out a gasp as pleasure overwhelms me, a twisted, filthy pleasure that I shouldn't enjoy, shouldn't like—but I do. I do.

My body clenches down on Aden. I come hard, crying out, and Aiden lets out a growl against my neck.

He fucks me hard and deep and frantic, his rhythm breaking up as he gets closer to his own orgasm. My head bangs against the wall, but I hardly notice. I come to another peak as Aden pushes in deep and comes inside me. I'm breathless with the heat and pleasure filling me all over again.

Finally, he exhales, panting. We stay against the wall until he unhooks my legs from around his hips one by one and lowers me back to the floor.

Aden leans his forehead against mine, catching his breath. He skims his hand over my waist, then slides his fingers between my legs to feel the mess he's left.

"I needed this," he says, his voice soft and gentle. "Never leave me."

We've been doing this for years. Ever since we found each other.

"Never," I promise him. "I need you too." I tell him, but I know, there's someone else who I need just as much.

CHAPTER 6

DEAN

It took me a long time to get used to having a routine again.

Once you have a routine like we did at that school, you'll never want one again. I rebelled when I got out. I hated everything and everyone. It was hell in my head. Didn't matter where my feet were anymore.

Everything we did was by a routine. Every single thing, including going to the bathroom some days. Routines like that are how they control us.

It's just as easy to fuck with people by fucking with the routine. That was part of the genius of it, if you could call it that. Sometimes the schedule would be so rigid and repetitive that going insane would have been a relief. They'd make us stick to the schedule no matter what, with plenty of punishments for anybody who screwed it up. They beat the schedule into us. Starved it into us. Screamed it into us. Anything they could think of.

Then it would turn on a dime.

Once they had us ready to die from boredom or monotony or the pain, they'd switch everything up again. Then the fear would keep us on our toes. Didn't make anything better. It just meant my heart would race all the time. Most nights I couldn't fall asleep. The nightmare of the day sleeping with me at night.

When they'd change the schedule, there was almost never any point in falling asleep. They'd just wake us up again. They did that to keep us desperate and focused on when we could lay down again. They did that to drive us insane. Like they wanted a fresh start so they'd break us down until we didn't know what was right and what was wrong.

It worked.

They wouldn't have done it if it didn't. Hell, they had success stories to brag about which led to all the federal money they scraped up.

God, they loved that schedule shit. It was the perfect way to control us. From the outside, nobody could argue with the schedule. We were troubled teens, so we needed boundaries and a routine we could rely on. Even when some of us tried to explain how it was—and it was never often, because parents weren't allowed to visit more than a couple times a year, and when they left, you ended up right back where you started. We were fucked if we tried to tell them anything, and even more fucked if our parents tried to talk to anyone at the school. The police even came once and the only thing that happened is that they arrested the kid. It was like everyone was against us and we really were so fucking bad to the core, that everyone wanted to hurt us. And they could get away with it, over and over again.

That was the kind of thing everybody learned fastest. Asking for help, or even seeming like you might need it, would only get you hurt, and usually pretty badly.

It was never worth it to explain.

Looking back, that was one of the sickest things they did. They made it seem like reaching out to anybody was the most dangerous thing we could do. That habit stuck. To this day, whenever I think about talking to somebody about something that's happening with me, I'm always making a mental list of the punishments I could get later.

And of the things they'd think about me.

I know they won't happen. I've done plenty of work on convincing myself that those things are just intrusive thoughts. They're not real anymore.

I think about them anyway, but they linger back in. That's why I needed to find her. My head is split and and sometimes I just can't think right. She gets it though. She was there. She knows.

I spent too long in a place where everything was controlled down to the minute and where that damn schedule would always be used against me. It's probably not a surprise that after I got out, I didn't want anything to do with a schedule. I didn't want to have to be anywhere at somebody else's beck and call. I skipped appointments and stood up what few friends I had left and fucked off for days at a time just because I could. And because it was better to be alone.

All that focus on the schedule backfired, obviously. What did that school claim it would do? Straighten us out. Make us productive citizens. Make us listen to our parents and get good grades and never cause any problems for the rest of our lives.

That's not what it did to me. I was angry, even if half the time I couldn't feel it. What made me most angry was somebody else deciding where I should go and when I should be there.

It took a long time to come around to the idea of having a job. Mechanics though... I've always found peace in that.

Found out I was good at it, too. After a couple of years of classes, I applied for a job at the garage next to my house. Spent a year working part time, then moved to full-time.

I keep to myself. I do my job.

Plus, the guys at the shop get it. It's not like I had a heart-to-heart with them about my past. I can't remember telling my boss, Rick, any specifics. Maybe he guessed somehow.

Maybe there was something about me that gave it away.

But they let me be. They give me my space. And they treat me like anyone else: a human being.

My boss and I have an understanding too. He knows it's better for me to pick my own hours and show up when I'm able. When the thoughts aren't so loud that I can focus. He doesn't box me in on a schedule or chew me out for coming in at different times depending on the day. He lets me have my way with it, and I repay him by working forty hours every week and putting in extra time when the other guys need days off or get sick. And I always get the job done on time. Even if I come in at 3 am because I can't sleep. He's fine with it.

With my hands in my checkered jacket pockets, and in my blue jeans which are already stained, I walk outside and lock up, ready to head to work. The air still smells fresh and dewy as I walk, and it's a bit crisp.

I walk into the shop a little after nine in the morning. It's full of familiar noises—wrenches clanging, guys shouting from the pit under the cars, the smell of oil, tires, and grease.

Rick, a barrel-chested guy in his early fifties, and wrinkles around his eyes that show every bit of his age, nods to me as he twists a rag around greasy fingers. He's already been in the guts of a car this morning. Knowing him, more than one. The man's a machine when it comes to fixing cars. He could charge a lot more, but he doesn't.

"How you doing, Dean?" he asks.

"Good. And you?" I keep it easy as I always do. Waiting for my list and ready to get lost in whatever car they give me.

"Good as I can be."

With a quick glance in the back I can see there's plenty to do. There almost always is.

The way people talk about Rick means he's never had to put an ad in the paper or post on websites or anything like that. People just keep coming back. They tell other people to come to our shop. That's the dream, really. Rick has a guaranteed job. That means I have a guaranteed job. It's steady income and I appreciate that.

One of the other guys comes to ask Rick a question. I pick up a clipboard hanging from a nail on the wall and look over the day's projects. I pick the one that's next up and get started, initialing next to it so they know I'm on it.

With that I head back, grabbing my overalls and minding my own business.

My hours go by like they do every day at the shop. I run down the list of repairs and squeeze in a little old lady's car when she doesn't have an appointment. She came in worried as hell about it—something to do with her groceries and having to shop on a certain day. She won't miss it. That's the kind of nice shit I never pictured when I was at that place. Why would I bother? Now it gives me the kind of satisfaction I never thought to want.

It's not that it makes me happy to be a good person, but it

is nice. Deep down inside, I'm not sure I could ever be a good person after the things I've done. Those thoughts are always there. They never leave, they just bury themselves deep down inside and let me have a moment to pretend.

In the afternoon, Rick calls it quits. He gets a list going for tomorrow and tells us we'll work on it then.

The last thing I do before I leave is strip off my coveralls and throw them in the pile with the other guys'. Rick has them washed all together. Too much oil and grease will fuck up a regular washer and dryer, so he takes care of that. I get a fresh coverall from the stack so I'll have it tomorrow morning, say my goodbyes, and head back down the sidewalk to my house.

A simple end to a simple day. I'm all set for tomorrow. Ready for the routine.

At home I wash the day off, scrubbing the stains out of my hands. The hot water crashing down on me, washing away every thought and my mind wanders to Haley. It always does.

I got rust under my fingernails somehow. It takes a solid five minutes with a fingernail brush to get them clean.

Then, once I've dressed in fresh clothes, I head to the bar. This is part of the routine that I chose, too. The bar itself is cozy and clean and only a few blocks from my house. The bartenders know my name and my face. One of them has my beer waiting when I slide onto a barstool, inhaling the peanut shells and beer and burgers.

My friend takes the stool next to me, accepts a beer from

the bartender, and nudges me with his elbow.

"Good day at work?"

"Good as it could be. You?" I answer like Rick does.

"Hell of a day, I'll tell you what."

He does tell me what. Michael tells me about some mix-up with a copy machine and somebody trying to order pizza from the appliance repair place he works at. As he talks, more of the regulars show up. We give each other shit for having boring jobs and take turns commenting on the game. I nurse the same beer the entire night. I've done it for years although I always order bottle after bottle. I just give it to someone else.

I like a buzz now and then, but I mostly come to the bar for the company and I don't trust not being in control. The guys aren't afraid to touch my shoulder or look me in the eye. That was the simplest thing they took from us at school. Couldn't look. Couldn't touch. Still feels like I'm getting away with something when it happens now.

They all do it now. Easy and comfortable like. With every touch I'm reminded and my hands stay on the bottle of beer. Picking at the label.

Picking. Picking. Picking. Sometimes I hear them, sometimes it changes to a loud ringing and the screams. All the screaming.

My phone vibrates in my pocket while I'm leaving money at my spot on the bar. Michael snags my elbow and tells me one more quick story, then lets me go.

The walk goes quicker on the way home.

I don't bother looking at my phone until I'm behind the wheel of my car. I already know what's going to be on the screen.

Sure enough, when I pull out my phone, the instructions are there waiting for me.

Reminder: Ridgemore. 3 am.

I start the car and let my mind go blank. I don't want to think. I don't want to remember anything—not even who I am.

The man I find in Ridgemore is the man that watched me piss. The one who used to constantly watch. He had a baton on his waist. I'm not sure whether his hands on that baton hit me the most. He's not ready for me. He doesn't hear me coming. Nobody does.

Nobody hears him when he starts to squeal, either. I hit him over the head with an old baseball bat I found in the dumpster a few months back so many times that it stops looking like a human head at all—just a mess.

By then, he's not making any sound.

By then, he's very still.

But I keep going. It only seems fair. It barely even feels real. The blood being hot as it splashes, the lights behind the trees from the cars on the street... none of it truly registers. In my head, I'm him, beating the shit out of me when I was only a fucking kid.

Lots of people have ideas about right and wrong. Most

would say that killing is wrong. But how could they think that when they did all that shit to us? And they were allowed to. No one ever got in trouble when the truth finally came out. They just got to go home. So right and wrong, when it comes to what other people think... well it doesn't really register for me.

I learned from that school that what people say isn't what they mean.

I learned that nothing matters except making sure everyone gets their punishment.

CHAPTER 7

DEAN

10 YEARS AGO

The "treatments" are never treatments in this hell hole. It's like everything else about the school. It's not really a school, it's a prison for people like me. Delinquents. Nuisances. Some of us did actually commit a crime and got caught. I know I've shoplifted before but I got away with it. It was just candy bars. It was wrong and I know that. It was stupid. That was last year when I was 14. My buddy Nick did it first and I know I shouldn't have. It was dumb and I was missing my mom.

Just thinking about her makes me want to cry. She wouldn't want this for me. She would have told Dad there was another way. Bad grades and acting dumb... I know I shouldn't have, but this?

I don't deserve this. No one fucking deserves this.

It's not a school, and the treatments aren't really treatments—they're just torture.

That's obvious after about an hour in this place, and it only gets more obvious as the days go by. If you stand in silence, perfectly still, just listening to the cries and screams, the things they tell us... it's not right. Nothing here is what it's supposed to be. I really do wonder how they sold this place to our parents. What the hell would they put on a brochure to make this seem like it would help?

It feels like my soul is chipping away piece by piece.

I wonder if they needed my dad's consent for the treatments, because I've been in *treatments* for months, and there's nothing to treat. Nobody in their right mind would call this medicine. Nothing about it will heal me. It'll only make things worse.

That's the goal. These people want to break me. They want to turn me into someone who follows orders at every cost.

I've been doing that already. They don't know how much it costs to feel like this, but then they don't care.

Mr. Jay cares least of all. I've been alone with him in this room for an hour. Maybe two. Maybe three. There's no clock, so there's no way for me to be sure what time it is. After dinner, I think. I try not to guess what time it is. Time doesn't matter anyway. You're up when they tell you to get up. If that's 3am or noon, it doesn't matter. If you got to bed at 9 and they say rise and shine at 10, you get your ass up or you get the shit beat out of you.

Besides, time doesn't pass normally here. I think it's been hours, so it's probably only been minutes. I think it's been years, so I've probably only been here for months.

It's better if I don't think about it.

Most of what's on my mind is that my stomach hurts.

It hurts because it's full of water. Mr. Jay said to drink a bottle when we first came in. Then another. Then another.

It's been hours and he keeps bringing in bottles to drink. I don't know how many so far. All I can remember is that it was warm and tasted like plastic, like it had been sitting in a case too long. I can't move from where I am. I can't let my back rest against the chair. I have to sit on the edge of it. The stack of books in my lap. My legs stiff.

I have to piss and I know he wants me to piss myself. To hurt and ache. To be weak and pathetic. I hold it in though. Silently sitting perfectly still. Staring ahead and trying not to cry when the baton comes down on the books.

This is because of what happened at dinner, which was...

I don't know what it was. Something one of the staff members didn't like. Might just have been my face being my face. I can't remember the details anymore. I'm not even completely sure I'm remembering the right dinner. All the days are starting to seem like the same day.

Maybe that's what they're trying to do. Fuck up our sense of time so badly that we don't know what year it is, or month.

The joke is on those bastards. I know it's the middle of the year because the room is hot. If it was fall or spring, the room would be freezing.

It's sweltering now. Sweat drips down my back.

"I have to use the bathroom."

"No you don't," he tells me and I close my mouth. I could scream. I could scream but then I'd be hit again.

"You need to answer the question correctly," he tells me, his tone condescending.

My ass has gone numb from sitting on the hard chair so long, my bladder full and my legs aching with the pressure of the stack of textbooks.

"What's the first rule that all students are required to follow?" Mr. Jay glances at the wall as he speaks like he might find a window there. Who knows? Maybe there's some window he can see that I can't.

I answer hoping to be done with this. "Rule number one." We've gone over this at least a hundred times. "Do not look at another student."

"What's the second rule all students are required to follow?"

"Rule number two. Do not make verbal contact with another student."

"What's the third rule all students are required to follow?"

"Rule number three. Do not—" My stomach lurches, and

I clamp my teeth together and swallow hard to stop myself from being sick or pissing myself. "Do not make physical contact with another student."

"What's the fourth rule all students are required to follow?"

He goes on through his list, and I go on through the rules. When he gets to the end of the list, he starts over at the first rule.

I nearly cry. My throat closing up and tears pricking my eyes.

"I have to pee." I tell him. "I'm going to piss myself," I confess.

"No you don't," he tells me and adds another book to the stack then presses them closer to my stomach.

I don't know why I'm being punished, and I know he won't tell me if I ask. The reason will come down to something I did wrong. Some word I didn't say right. Some attitude I had while I was answering. It's not like I can forget the rules. I could repeat them in my sleep, and sometimes I dream about having to recite them in places they don't belong, like a gas station or at the movie theater. Like one day I might get out of here. Although I'm starting to lose hope.

"The rules," he says. "When you break the rules we have to break them into you."

Biting my tongue, I resist the urge to ask which one I've broken. My mind instantly goes to the girl. The vision of her.

I haven't even seen her. I don't know her name. It's like he knows my thoughts. It's not a rule though, I'm allowed to think of her. She's the only thing keeping me sane. The desire to know she's okay.

He asks again and I answer the damn questions.

"—make verbal contact with another student," I say. My stomach is so tight with all the water. If I was anywhere else, I would've been sick by now. That's something I can't do in this room with this man. If I throw up, he'll probably start over and we'll be here for another year, me listing out a sadistic monster's idea of school rules and Mr. Jay looking bored.

My stomach lurches, and I swallow.

Swallow.

Swallow again.

Am I going to throw up or piss myself? I don't know which he's after. I don't know which will get me the worst punishment either.

"I have to throw up," I tell him, leaning forward and the books slip, my leg cramps.

I'm not sure when he starts to hit me. The blows seem like they're coming from far away. We go back to the beginning of the list and through the whole thing again. At first, he hits me with an open hand, but that must be boring, too, because he switches to a fist.

Why does he do it? I don't know. I guess it probably makes some kind of sense to the people who run this place, but it will never make sense to me. There's just no reason for him to do this. It's not even worth my time to figure it out.

My head is so fucked, I can barely make sense of the room.

It spins and goes fuzzy. Everything does. I'm here but I'm not.

I'm also not sure when I stop...being there.

I'm still in the room. There's no escape from this place, so my body stays on the chair. I don't try to get away from Mr. Jay's fist. I know where I am, just like I know the rules are taped to the wall opposite me. The print is too small for me to read them, but I don't need the paper to tell me what they are.

My mouth moves, but it belongs to someone else. The longer I talk, the more I feel like someone else is talking for me.

The longer Mr. Jay hits me, the more it feels like he's hitting someone else.

That's been happening more often lately, I think. I exist in my body, but I don't. The school exists around me, but it doesn't. As I sit in the chair, answering Mr. Jay's questions, I start to imagine another place.

I don't imagine much at first. For a while, all I can picture is a sidewalk. It's a regular sidewalk with some cracks in the concrete and grass on either side. It's not like the patches of sidewalk in front of the school that don't lead anywhere. This sidewalk leads to somewhere else—I know it.

Eventually, it becomes a street with houses and yards in the front. It's not some half-abandoned place with one building in the middle of nowhere. It's a neighborhood.

A nice neighborhood, with people who aren't sick bastards in it. People who check up on each other to make sure they're okay. Dads who mow the lawn on the weekends. Moms who go shopping on Wednesdays.

A fucking paradise, right?

I imagine walking down that sidewalk until the middle of the street. That's when I stop and go into a house.

This isn't my dad's house. This is my house. I live here, and nobody else can get in. I can shut the door and flip the lock, and they can't touch me. The living room has carpet, not concrete, and the furniture's simple and clean. I'm safe here.

In this house, there's a picture window in the living room. It's not some bullshit prison privacy glass. It's a normal window I can see out of, with curtains that I can close if I want. If I don't, I can let the sun in. I could break that window with my bare hands, if I wanted, because it's not safety glass.

In this house, I don't want to break the window. I don't need to. None of the people who run the school exist anymore.

Is this a daydream?

Guess it doesn't matter.

In the daydream, or whatever it is, I sit down on the sofa in my living room and watch the sidewalk outside the house. People walk by. Little kids and teenagers and parents. All kinds of people.

And then she's there.

She's so fucking beautiful.

She's beautiful even at this school, but in the sun, she looks incredible. Everything's better in the sun. We're older. Just old enough that no one can force us to be where we don't want to be.

The girl must feel me watching, because she stops on the sidewalk and looks in. She meets my eyes and waves.

If I wanted, I could go out to her. I could talk to her. Nobody can punish me for that here.

I can do whatever I want. And none of this happened. I never learned the rules so I can look her in the eyes and it's okay.

I could touch her, even. I could find out what her skin feels like under my hands. I could find out how warm she is. They couldn't stop me. Nobody could stop me.

Somebody shakes my shoulder. Violently, in a bruising forceful way.

"Fucking pay attention when I speak to you!" he screams and it's then I feel the blood on my lip, wait no, my nose. My nose bleeds and the pounding in my head gets worse.

Fuck, it hurts. I'm going to throw up.

I don't answer. It doesn't seem like he's talking to me. *Where am I?*

Eventually, I move my eyes and look at his face. Mr. Jay glares at me like I'm the one who kept us in here for so long.

He scoffs. "You're done."

I don't bother to hope. I know he doesn't mean that I'm done here at the school. They'll never let me out. They've made that clear. I'm too worthless and stupid to be let out of this place. I'll never tell them exactly what they want to hear, so they'll never send me anywhere else.

"Done?" I ask. My mouth feels tacky and dry.

He leans in close, his eyes nearly black with anger. "Done for the night. You've wasted enough of my time. Get up you fucking animal."

I can't. My stomach is in knots. My legs feel weak. In some faraway part of my brain, I'm still in the neighborhood. I'm still looking out at the girl through my front window. For once, it's not a cage. She's outside in the sunlight, and I can look at her as much as I want.

Mr. Jay's fingers dig into my arm. He escorts me through the hall—dragging me, really, and muttering things under his breath.

We stop outside the staff bathroom. He bangs in through the door, leaving me in the hall.

When I first got here, I might have seen this as an opportunity to try to run away. Now I know there's no point. I won't get to the front doors. Even if I did, there's miles of empty land between me and the nearest place I could go for help.

The teachers would find me.

I turn my head, and there she is.

For a few seconds, I think I've gone back into my daydream. Maybe my mind really has split off and I exist there now.

The girl sits in a chair with no desk in front of it, her hands folded in her lap, her eyes bright despite the lack of light in the hall or in the room.

That's the room they take people to for punishment. When they want to hurt somebody so bad there's no record of what they've done. That's the room with no cameras.

I stare at her face, hungry for the sight of her.

Her dark hair is a mess on one side, like she hasn't brushed it in days. Her skin is pale, even her lips. She doesn't look like she did. She's sick now like me. Fuck. Everything twisted in knots inside of me get tighter. Not her.

I stare at her but she doesn't look up. She doesn't see me. *She'll never see me.*

I can't stand the thought. She has to see me. I almost say something. I swear there's a whisper of a question: what's your name? On my lips.

I'm breaking rule number one, and I'll pay for it. If Mr. Jay steps out of the bathroom behind me, he'll take me back to the room we just left. He might even punish me in front of the girl, in the room with no cameras.

I don't care. I can't stop.

Water runs in the staff bathroom. I have a few more seconds. The girl stares back at me, completely still, not making a sound. I know she sees me, though. Her eyes get a little brighter. Her breathing is a little quicker.

She *sees* me.

My stomach lurches again and my head gets light. I'm forced to lean against the brick wall. It's fucking freezing. Suddenly everything is freezing.

The bathroom door opens with a creak behind me and I stand up straight, holding back bile. I turn my head forward and let my face fall into an emotionless mask. I don't move a muscle, as if I've been staring forward the entire time Mr. Jay has been in the bathroom.

I can feel her eyes burning into my skin.

My heart beats loud in my ears. Another few seconds stretch by. All I want to do is look back at her but I don't.

One day. One day we'll be out of here. But I don't know if I can wait that long. If they're doing to her what they do to me... They have to be stopped. She can't turn into what I am. They can't do that to her. I won't let them.

CHAPTER 8

HALEY

PRESENT DAY

The woman who sits across from me in my office reminds me of something from school.

I can't put my finger on who it was, exactly. For a long time, every name I learned there was burned into my brain. That's what happens when you're not allowed to get to know anyone else. Those pieces of information are precious and forbidden, so I held them close to my chest.

I remember very clearly how I felt about the things we weren't allowed to have, like food and privacy and friendships. An opinion. A voice. Whenever I learned something about another student, I hoarded it. Unlike food, those facts couldn't go bad.

Kelly. My patient's name is Kelly. As far as I know, there was no Kelly at the school. I memorized every name after we got out. When the files were released, we saw everything unfold.

It's not her name that reminds me. I think it's the color of her hair—a dark, natural brunette. The way it's parted not quite down the center and the softness of her curls.

She looks just like her. I know the girl's face from the black and white photos better than the memories from that school. She's one of the ones who killed herself.

I take a deep breath, my notebook shifting on my lap and I steady myself. Now is not the time to be sifting through old memories of that place. Now is the time to focus on my patient.

To focus on Kelly.

We're forty minutes into the session, and she is curled into an overstuffed chair across the office from me. Her posture is defensive and hurt.

In my experience, there are two ways people can go when they look like that. Kelly might be on the edge of a breakthrough, or she might be on the edge of getting up and walking out.

I would understand if she did. I've done my fair share of walking out of appointments when it seemed like the therapist I was working with would never understand.

Now I know that it's impossible for people who weren't in that situation at the school with us to understand, and I don't blame them.

Kelly sniffles. Tears run down her face, but she clears her throat, her expression determined.

"Take your time," I reassure her and she heaves in a breath, her fingers running through her hair and then resting on her forehead.

I'm glad for all the work I put into my office at times like this. I wanted it to look safe and welcoming. I wanted it to *be* safe and welcoming, of course. Some therapists think the environment isn't the most important thing when it comes to working with patients, but I don't know where they got that idea. Kelly's shoulders relaxed the first time she stepped into my office. She's never said what the furniture and the soft lighting—light from the window during the day—and the throw blanket on the arm of the overstuffed chair reminds her of. She might not even know on a conscious level.

But I'm glad that the space around her is comfortable, because she's clearly experiencing some uncomfortable feelings.

"I'm here to listen," I remind her. "I'm interested to know how you're feeling and what you're thinking about right now."

"Ugh," she says. "I'm frustrated. I'm so frustrated, and I don't know what—"

Kelly breaks off and whips another tissue from the box on the side table. She blows her nose, then crumples the tissue into a tiny ball in her fist.

I wait, one leg crossed over the other, keeping my body relaxed. It enrages me that people can hurt other people the way Kelly has been hurt and the way I've been hurt. I don't let myself get angry when I'm in sessions. I don't let it show. I keep it in a little tin box, locked away with a tiny key deep down inside of me until the door is closed and the patient is gone.

Kelly looks toward the window, breathing deeply. Her cheeks reddened, and when she looks back at me, that betrayal is reflected in her eyes.

"It just feels like it keeps coming back," she presses, the frustration lingering in her voice.

My throat gets tight… I know that feeling.

"I feel like," Kelly begins, her voice thick with truth and emotion. "No matter how far away I get, no matter how much time passes, it's still there." She points at her chest. "Like it's in my body, waiting for the moment I feel good, or I feel like I'm past it, or—" Kelly drops her hand to her lap, the tissue still clenched in her fist. "The second I let my guard down, it's waiting to pounce on me again. Almost like it's playing with me. Almost like *I'm* playing with me, because these are my— this is how I feel about what he did. I keep thinking I'm over it. But then something will happen and I'm right back in that house. All I want is to erase it somehow, and…I don't know how to do that."

"Where in your body do you feel that?" I ask her and she taps on her chest three times. "Right here," she admits with her eyes glassy, "and sometimes my throat gets tight."

I nod. "There's a book I can recommend to you. You're not wrong. The body holds trauma, and you don't have resolution or justice. It's hard on the body when there was never an ending that makes you feel safe."

She lets out a heavy sigh. Her eyes drop to her hands in her lap, her lip quivering. Kelly grits her teeth and the dimple in her chin disappears.

I sit with what she's said for a few moments.

I don't want to rush to respond to her. I want her to know that I've considered her words before I start talking.

And—

The way she said *back in that house* jogged something in my brain. That's how I would've said *back at school*. That's how I think *back at school* in my own head.

My mind races and I remind myself that I need to stop. It's only the news and the recent events that have brought all of this up.

"It's your grief and you're allowed to acknowledge that you feel that way. You can process it just like you are. Talking through it. The more you do, the easier it will come and the easier it will feel."

She tries to respond but can't, I look at the 20-year-old like she is me. That's how I used to lay when I was struck with the past and could barely move, let alone talk about it.

I know the situation isn't the same. What happened to

Kelly with her ex-boyfriend was just as wrong as what was done to us in school, but there are some differences that I've been careful to acknowledge.

One similarity is that it wasn't our fault. What happened to me happened because of my parents, and in another way, it happened because of the people who lied to my parents.

What happened to Kelly happened because of her boyfriend. It was his choice to act the way he did.

I think Kelly is at a place where she's ready to see her own power again. That can be extremely hard, but without it, some people don't feel that their lives are worth living.

"Kelly." I keep my voice soft and my notebook and pen down. This is something I want to say to her directly, and I want her to hear it from me directly. I look her in the eyes, and her expression brightens with tentative hope. "Everything that happens—good or bad—has an impact. Sometimes it's harder to see the changes that good things bring, but they affect us just like the bad things. All our experiences shape us this way. We're constantly growing and constantly learning, and we're all a little different every day because of what happens to us and because of how we deal with it. Those are the things that make us who we are. And you are coping the best you can and you're taking steps. These are things to be proud of."

She swallows, the cords in her neck tightening, "The only thing that makes sense is to pretend it didn't happen or forget about it somehow. How else am I supposed to leave it in the past?"

"You don't."

Kelly's doe eyes go wide.

"You can't leave it behind because you can't leave *you* behind. I know it hurts to have this with you. I know you're suffering, otherwise you wouldn't be here. If you could forget or pretend it didn't happen, you'd be out there living your life and not trying to work through this."

Kelly makes a helpless gesture, speechless at my suggestion.

"I think the only way to leave these experiences in the past—in any shape or form—is to accept that they happened and accept that they changed you. And then, when old feelings come up again, remember that you survived them once. Acknowledge the pain. Process your feelings and talk it through. They might feel as strong as they did when it first happened, but the difference now is that they can't control you. You got away from your ex-boyfriend. He can't ever change the things he did or the way he made you feel. But you can choose how you live from now on."

Kelly looks at me for a long moment, her lips pressed into a thin line.

"You're the one who makes decisions about your life now," I press on. "You decide what you'll do, no matter how you feel. You have control over your life. You do. I know it doesn't always feel like that, but you do. You can choose what to do with those feelings."

"What if I just ignore them? Just choose not to feel them?" She leans slightly into the arm of the chair, pulling her legs up. Her arms wrap around her jeans and the sleeves of her thin sweater fall over her hands. Her blue eyes beg me to lie to her. I can't do it though. I won't ever hurt someone like that.

"I'm not sure that's going to work; it hasn't yet, right?" I answer and her expression crumples. She moves the tissue to the corner of her eyes as I talk. "Acknowledge them—and then make your own decision. Whatever harm you suffered, whatever damage other people did, that's the end of their power over you. You can decide to move forward however you want." She reaches for another tissue and the sun sets slightly behind her, darkening the room. I add, "It might take time, and it might be difficult, but you can make those choices. You do have a choice to make, even when it doesn't feel like it. Even when it feels harder to have a choice."

She's silent, absorbing my words.

"So, at work," she says slowly, "when it comes up again—"

We go through the situations at work that send her spiraling. We talk out different ways to respond and methods for centering herself so she *can* respond instead of reacting to what happens. We spend the last part of the session making plans for what Kelly can do at work and with her friends and with her family to remind herself that she has control. Not over everyone, but over how she chooses to respond.

Kelly doesn't like the idea of sitting with panic or grief until those feelings aren't so intense, but she comes around to it. "There's no shame in walking away and taking a moment before responding to someone or to a situation."

"Better than having a breakdown," she finally admits. "Even if I hate it."

I offer her a small smile. "Sometimes I hate it, too. Feelings are like that, especially when they're related to trauma."

When Kelly heads for the door, she's standing up straighter and her eyes are dry. Her chin is lifted. She looks far more hopeful than she did when she walked in.

"Thank you," she says. "Thank you. That really helped."

"You're welcome," I say. "I'll see you in two weeks."

I watch her go, feeling hopeful, too.

That feeling doesn't last very long after Kelly has shut the door behind her and the sound of her car engine has faded.

I'm left with a sinking feeling in my stomach. It's a very uncomfortable feeling, and one that I know well.

All of those things I told Kelly about how the past can't control her—I needed to hear those, too. They're the same things I heard many times before they sunk in.

I guess I forgot. I guess I haven't been doing as well as I thought. My hands tremble and I busy them by grabbing a tissue from the box on the coffee table.

Tears have gathered in the corners of my eyes without me

noticing, and I feel a release in my chest, as if I've been trying to tell myself about my own power and my own control, but I wasn't getting through. Maybe it took telling someone else to hear them again.

The school...the things they did there...I don't have to let it control me. I can't be blamed, of course, for the crimes of other people. And for suffering the way I did. I can't even blame myself for how the feelings come back and how I forget that those days are long gone, and I'll never be at the mercy of those kinds of people again.

"I can choose," I tell myself in my empty office. "I can choose what to do. I have power over my life."

I repeat them a few more times until they seem settled in my head, then wipe away a few tears with a tissue.

As I toss my tissues into the small trash can by my desk, it starts to vibrate.

It's not actually the desk or the plastic bin vibrating. It's my phone in one of my desk drawers.

I take a breath and open the drawer. On the screen is my friend Michaela's name. My chest lightens at the sight of it. I almost let it go to voicemail, but I answer it, praying for a distraction.

"Hi, girl." I read somewhere that you should smile when you answer the phone because the other person can hear it. I force a smile and keep my voice uplifted. "What's going on?"

"Not much," Michaela must be smiling, too. I can picture

it like she's right in front of me. "I was just thinking about you. We haven't talked in a while. How are you?"

"I'm fine," I blurt out, my voice falsely high. Why? I *am* fine. "I'm doing great. Did something happen?"

"No," Michaela says. "No, I just had a feeling that I should call you, so I picked up the phone. It's funny. I was just walking by a house that reminded me of your old neighborhood. Do you remember that playground we used to go to?" She laughs.

"Of course," I answer, but the hairs on the back of my neck stand up. I move away from the window on instinct, but then I turn to face it and look through the curtains. "Why?"

She answers something about nostalgia but I can't listen, let alone speak. There's a flash of a man outside my window.

A man, well a boy, I remember very well from school. He's only visible for a few seconds before he disappears behind a building across the street.

My entire body erupts in chills and for a moment I swear I think I'm seeing things.

It can't have been him. Maybe I'm just imagining that I saw him. It's like Kelly—she reminded me of someone I used to know, but that person isn't here. My heart rampages as Michaela drones on.

I step closer to the window, moving the curtain to the side. There's no one there. Nothing but the wind blowing the branches. Michaela is still talking, but I've lost track of what she's saying.

There's nothing there. Even still I close the blinds and let out a small laugh along with Michaela... what the hell we're laughing over, I don't know.

"Anyway," she says, "you should come out tonight. I'd love to see your face."

"I'll think about it," I promise, and end the call. My hands trembling and my mind taken back ten years ago.

CHAPTER 9

HALEY

10 YEARS AGO

Don't move.

Don't move a muscle.

Don't blink or breathe too hard or give any sign that you want to run away.

I keep the thoughts in my head on a loop. There are no other games to play in this place. The only place I can escape to is inside my head.

Don't move. Stay perfectly still.

It's late at night, but without a clock, I don't know what time it is. My body is tired, my muscles ache in a way I didn't think was possible. They make us do jumping jacks all day long until our legs can't stand then the next day, still as can be. We're not allowed to move.

I've been sitting at this narrow desk for so long. I run through the alphabet, and count to a hundred. I think of every song I know but I'm careful not to move my lips.

I try to think of something else to pass the time, but there's nothing there in my head.

I go through the colors of the rainbow.

My heart pounds hard and fast. It won't slow down no matter how long I sit here on this side of a one-sided mirror. On the other side— I refuse to think. I refuse to believe it's real.

I just ignore it.

I count to ten again, then twenty.

The man keeps shouting at me. He's been shouting for so long that I think his voice is starting to break down. His throat must be raw and hurting.

The quiet isn't any better.

It just means I can hear the grunts from the other side of the window, and the sound of Mr. Jay's boot coming down on the boy's hand. The screams. Tears prick my eyes.

I try to ignore it. The door is locked. I can't do anything. They want me to watch so I keep my head straight but I try not to see what's right in front of me.

We shouldn't have looked at each other. We shouldn't have said hello.

We broke the rules for what?

For both of us to get beaten one at a time, in front of each other. My punishment was first. And my body is still shaking. My throat worse off from screaming.

And my hands, I look down at them black and blue. I shouldn't have done anything.

I wonder if there's anything left of the girl I once was.

My heart. That's what's left. It beats hard, like it's trying to warn me but this is wrong. My heart still knows that this is sick and terrible and a good person would intervene.

I'm not a good person.

Maybe I never was.

I'm not going to get out of my chair. I'm not going to go to bang at the door and scream for help. I added the time to his beatings. It's my fault. It's all my fault.

He might break the boy into pieces.

Don't move.

Don't move a muscle.

I don't even dare to close my eyes.

It's twisted—all I can think is how I'm breaking the rules. I'm not supposed to look at any other student for any reason. But I have to look at the boy. They decided that I have to break the rules.

I hate them. I hate them all in a way I didn't think was possible. I don't understand how someone can cause so much pain and agony and then continue to live.

We have to get out of here. Before I turn to something else.

We have to listen to them, though.

We have to stay still and quiet and do as we're told.

We have to obey to get out. It's the only way.

I don't even know the man on the other side. I've never seen him before.

There's a small prick at my finger, like a needle almost. I nearly touch it. I nearly pick at it. Instead I press the tips of my fingers into the desk. My knuckles turn white and my hands go numb as I watch the boy get his punishment.

I don't know his name either. This poor boy I dared to look at. This boy I dared to speak to. I thought we were alone. My throat dries and I wish I could tell him.

The pain in my throat is unbearable and I don't know if it's from the screams or from not being able to talk.

Maybe I am crazy, but if I am, it's because the school has made me that way. If I expected everything to make sense, I probably would've died by now.

That sounds dramatic. I might have, though. Other girls have disappeared in the night, and when we wake up, their beds are empty. No one will say where they went or whether they're okay. I pray they got away.

They were good. Not like me. They listened. Unlike me.

The boy doesn't look at me and I'm grateful. It would only make me cry harder.

"Straighter," a voice from behind tells me, fingers digging into my shoulder. I sit up and watch. "That's better," the voice says and I stifle a gasp as the man sits the boy in the chair.

He drags both the boy and the chair, the metal legs screeching. I silently pray that he doesn't put him in front of me but he does. He can't see me, I tell myself. But I can see him. Beaten and bruised.

"You did that," the voice says and I don't know if it's the one behind me or the voice in my head. I know better than to respond to either.

I go through the alphabet again, letter by letter, and count slowly to one hundred.

I wish my mom was here. For the first time in what feels like months, I wish she was here to stop them.

It must've been something terrible.

It must've been something that kept them up at night. That scared my mom enough to send me away.

"Corporal punishment is the only thing that works with delinquents like you," the man says.

Blood drips from the boy's lip as he lifts his head and I swear he's going to talk back. He's going to say something, but he doesn't. The only way I can stop looking at the boy is to close my eyes, but I'm not allowed to close my eyes.

My heart hammers and I memorize his face. Every detail. I swallow thickly and I pray for the guard to say the boy's name.

Time ticks on. Not minutes, but hours. Hours of sitting there, watching him forced to sit and stare at the mirror on the wall.

They did it to me first. How long has it been?

There's a ringing in my ear and I can't hear. Please don't

ask me to repeat what he's saying. I pray, my heart racing.

"Are you listening?" He sticks his fingers in his hair and pulls. The boy's face crumples. "Are you listening to me?"

"Yes, sir," the boy answers. He speaks. His voice. I'll remember it forever. I can barely breathe as I watch.

He screams at the boy who tears up but doesn't cry. I wish he would, if he would give in, maybe the man will stop.

It will never end.

It will never, ever end.

The voice tells me.

"You're worthless!" The man screams. "You're completely worthless. You shouldn't exist. Nothing about you should exist. There's nothing that makes you worthwhile. I don't even think you can understand that. I don't think you can do what you came here to do. What did you come here to do?"

"Learn, sir," he answers. "And follow the rules." I know what will happen if I react. I know what will happen if I cry.

On the other side of the window, the boy twists his head at an angle that has to hurt. His eyes meet mine again. I thought my heart couldn't beat any faster, but it does.

I remind myself he can't see me.

How can he be so defiant after that?

How can he be so unbroken?

How can he risk it?

"You're nothing," the man repeats. "You're nothing to anyone. Nobody can fix you. Nobody should waste their time."

Tears stream down my cheeks and behind me the guard shifts his weight. I stay perfectly still. Desperate for this to be over.

Don't move.

Don't move a muscle.

I don't know how long it goes on.

At some point, I realize I'm back in the dorm, sleeping with my arm out over the side of the bed. It's not comfortable. My arm usually falls asleep.

But it doesn't matter how uncomfortable it is. That's the rule. We have to keep an arm out so—

I don't really know why. Probably so that it's hard to sleep. Or so they can drag us out of bed easier.

I don't know I've fallen asleep until the man I've never met shakes my shoulder, forcing me to wake. His face is mostly in shadows, but I know him. My heart races once again, like waking up from a terror.

"You'll give in," he says, obviously not caring if he wakes up the rest of the people in the dorm. "We'll win in the end. We always win. Why is that?"

My mouth is dry, but he won't leave until he has an answer.

"Because I'm worthless."

"That's right. You're worthless, and you're not going to win."

He stands and leaves me there, terrified and unable to think of anything other than what I did to the boy. It's my fault. Never again.

Never. Ever. Again.

CHAPTER 10

DEAN

The grime that covers my hands adds to my annoyance.

I don't like that feeling. I don't like when my hands are dirty at all, but—

It's not oil or grease from the shop. It's not even dirt on my hands from pulling weeds out of the ground at my house.

It's blood.

I hold my hands up in front of my face. There's not much light—just a streetlight and the moon—but the streaks all over my hands look black. My heart beats a bit faster at the realization.

That's blood.

There's more of it all over me. On my jeans and my shirt. I pat my face. Blood on my face, too, but I don't think it's mine.

I checked myself over. No wounds. I'm sore, but nobody stabbed me or shot me. I'm sure I would feel that.

Where did the blood come from? There's a faint light that spills into the alley way. I look around as my vision clears, searching for clues.

I feel like I've been running. I can't catch my breath. My lungs burn like I ran for miles, but—

Where am I? Fuck!

I flex my hands again. My knuckles are sore and slightly bruised. My entire body aches, actually. My thighs hurt and my core. What did I do? Get tackled? There's nobody here with me. I wait a moment, listening, but all I can hear is my own heavy panting.

Adrenaline courses through my veins, making me alert and awake, but why?

I check again, searching up and down the alley. Nobody's here. It's quiet aside from the sounds of cars far off. There are some very distant voices that sound like people coming out of the bar.

I blink harder, trying to get my bearings. This is an alley near my house. Closer to the bar, though. A few blocks past. I could've walked here.

Did I walk here? If I did, I can't remember it at all.

Jesus. Why am I so out of breath? Did I run here? Was I running from someone or chasing after someone? I hunch down, my palms on my knees. And as a couple walks past the opening, I hide in the shadows. What the fuck happened?

Shit. Shit. Shit!

I had to be doing something here. Did I go to the bar? My tongue doesn't taste beer, so I probably wasn't at the bar, or if I was, I was there hours ago. I don't feel like I usually do after a drink with the guys.

Jesus. What day is it even?

"Dean?" Her voice startles me.

Shit. I wipe my hands down on my jeans, and turn my back to her. "Yeah?" I call. "You okay?"

"Dean, what—" Her footsteps move closer. "What are you doing here?"

"I know, I—"

A woman I know walks out, her hair pulled back and her eyes wide. The girl my Dad wants to meet.

Her gasp cuts me off. "Dean, what happened? Oh my God. Did you hurt yourself?" Concern is etched in every syllable.

She reaches out frantically and takes my hand. It's still covered in blood. Wiping it off didn't do any good.

She turns it over with a gentle touch. "What happened?" I watch her face, filled with shock as she glances between my hand and my shirt and then finally looks me in the eyes. I swallow thickly.

"I don't know," I admit. Fear washes through me. Fear of what she'll know, of what she'll think of me… of what I'll have to do.

Her eyes move over my face and my clothes and her mouth presses into a thin line. Just then the dark sky opens and a light rain gathers. She pulls her light jacket tighter around herself. The dew drops gathering on her coat and in her dark brunette hair.

I don't know how, but understanding passes between us.

"Let's go," she says quietly. Keeping my hand in hers, she leads the way out of the alley and quickly down the street. She hustles to keep up with my gait and we stay on the sidewalk on the opposite street that's mostly residential, lacks streetlights, and barely a soul is out on this side of the street.

Questions race through my mind. It's all too much. It's like a whirlwind in my mind with nothing sitting still long enough for me to think clearly about anything.

What was I doing over here? How did she know to find me? Who's fucking blood is on me?

I don't ask any questions. I just go with her, matching her fast, determined pace. She looks all around us as we go back to my house. Her hand is tight on mine.

Protecting me. Her... protecting me. My gut twists and a voice in the back of my head screams that I'm pathetic. It sounds like him. Like Mr. Jay and the other guards. Their voices chase me down the street, urging me to walk faster and get home. Where I can lock the door and just try to think. Try to remember.

Nobody's following us that I can see. Although the

adrenaline coursing through my veins makes my hands tremble.

I'm still a little shaken up about finding myself in that alley by the time she opens my door, and once we're in, she closes and locks it. I watch her as she stares at the locked door a moment longer and then faces me.

My chest is still heaving and I don't know what to say or how to explain a damn thing.

I try to remember her name and at this moment, I can't. That causes more panic in me, so much so I can't help but to bring my hands to my hair and walk away.

What the fuck is wrong with me?

Her hand brushing my shoulder makes me pull back and I swallow hard before turning to face her. She's a good foot shorter than me. Those wide eyes stare up at me, still riddled with concern. Her nose wrinkles with sympathy.

"Come with me. It won't do us any good to stand here."

My eyes roam over her face as she takes my hand in hers. *What's her name?*

I remember her head tossed back against the wall and the arch of her throat and the sounds she made as I filled her again and again. I remember the way she said my name and how her fingernails bit into my skin through my shirt.

In the bathroom, she flicks the light on. We both wince. I look even worse in the mirror. There's a lot more blood than I thought.

Where did it come from?

How did I get this much blood all over me?

My pulse pounds in my ears as I wait for her to ask questions I don't know the answer to. But she doesn't.

"Okay," she says briskly. "Let me help you out of your clothes. We need to get you cleaned up." She drops her coat first, and wipes her hair back, slightly damp from the rain.

She starts the shower for me and sticks her hand in to make sure the temperature is right. She nods to herself. She's going to take care of me.

I stand in disbelief for a moment and then start to unbutton my shirt. The flannel is damp at my shoulders.

She glances down at the ground at my shoes. I follow her gaze. They appear clean. No blood that I can tell. "That's good, I think. You can hop in, and I'll deal with your clothes."

I strip down, watching her watch me and it's eerie how I'm able to compare between then and now. When I was just a kid and had to do the same.

The memories haunt me and I try to push them away, but they scream at me to remember. *How could I forget? What's her name?*

She has my bloody clothes in a little bundle in her arms. I wonder if she's pretending to be okay.

She looks into my eyes and offers me a thin smile as steam from the shower flows into the room.

"Get in," she says gently. "I'll be here when you're done."

She leaves the bathroom for a few minutes, and then the door opens. I can hear her rummaging around in my medicine cabinet.

Water sluices down over my hair and my body, tinged red. It flows down the drain. The blood is disappearing before my eyes. Once it's all gone, I hope it's like it never existed.

"Do you have any cuts?" she asks from outside the curtain. I shake some water out of my ears and add shampoo. "Should I get some Neosporin? It doesn't look like you have any in here, but I think that place on the corner is open all night. I bet they'd have some."

"No," I answer, my throat tight with emotion. "I'm okay."

The water stings my knuckles, but that's it. The sore muscles I have could be from work today. My memories of that are fuzzy, but it was probably like any other day. None of this seems like something to worry about.

Except the blood. That obviously wasn't mine. Is she still going to be this calm when she comes to the same realization?

Thump, thump. My heart pounds.

"Let me help you." She leans in through the shower curtain and takes my hands in hers. She has a washcloth and runs it gently over all the spots that might be sore, concentrating hard. "I'm sorry if this hurts," she murmurs. "I know how much they hurt your hands."

She looks down at my body and doesn't say anything. She simply continues to wash me down.

I murmur an answer, "They're okay."

"They might be okay now, but I don't want to cause you any more pain."

"I know you don't." As the spray comes down I meet her eyes and there's nothing but compassion there. "I'm alright." I give her a smile. "Just need to wash up."

I shampoo my hair twice and scrub every inch of myself with tons of suds. The water is running clear over me by the time I turn off the shower.

When I pull the curtain back I see she left a towel for me on the towel rack.

It's warm to the touch like she put it in the dryer. And on the sink there's a set of clothes.

"You all dry?" she calls when I open the bathroom door. "Here. Give me your towel."

I hand it over but don't let go and her eyes meet mine as she tries to take it.

"Sorry," she whispers. "This can't be an easy night." She takes my towel and goes up on tiptoes to kiss my cheek. I almost ask her what happened. I almost ask if she knows but I don't. I just let it be. I slip on the fresh T-shirt and boxers and she's still standing there, watching. I know she sees that I'm not the one who bled all over me.

She doesn't say anything though, not at first.

"Just give me a minute, okay? I'm going to take care of the bathroom."

I'll give her whatever she wants.

She disappears into the bathroom as I head to the kitchen. I get a beer out of the fridge and crack it open. It's pitch black out now and I only realize that when the light from the fridge fills the room.

I pause after closing the door and try to remember.

There are soft noises from inside my bathroom—liquid pouring out of a container. When she comes out a few minutes later, she smells like bleach, and her face is calm.

"All clean," she says, her voice warm and reassuring. "Everything's all good." Her voice cracks slightly but she keeps her expression warm.

She comes to where I stand at the kitchen counter and stands, waiting for something, and I open my arms. She snuggles into my chest, pressing her face into my shirt.

"It's alright," she whispers, "everything's just fine." She wraps her arms around my waist and holds me tight. The scent of her washes over me and I kiss her hair. My heart beating in time with hers.

We stand like that for a while. I don't like not knowing what happened. My body doesn't like it, either. It shakes in response to my nerves and I weather a few more waves of adrenaline.

Flashes of what feel like memories resurface but they're gone before I can make sense of them.

Haley holds me tighter and murmurs things in my ear.

Finally, she takes a deep breath and squeezes me close, then leans back so she can look into my eyes.

Her eyes hold so much emotion.

"I know this is hard," she says. "But you know I love you, and—"

I cut her off with a kiss.

Her arms come up to my neck, and she lets her weight hang off me. I need all of me closer to her, so I put my hands under her ass and lift her up, turning us around so I can put her on the counter. I want to get lost in her touch. Lost in a night of pleasure and lust and whatever else this is that I feel.

She lets out another gasp as I go for her clothes. The denim rubs against her thighs as I get her pants down and off, and then her panties, and then I cover her mouth with mine and kiss her deep while I find her clit with my fingertips.

"You're already wet. God, you're perfect."

She moans, the words muffled by our kiss. "Please. Please fuck me, Dean. Please. I need you."

I shove down my boxers, meaning to take her the second I can, but instead I drag my crown through her folds, teasing the both of us and using the tip to put pressure on her clit.

She makes low noises in the back of her throat, squirming on the countertop, clinging to my shoulders.

"Please," she moans. "Please, I'll give you anything you need. Please, I just need you." She slips her hands up my shirt and her nails scratch along my skin. Fuck, I need this.

I nip her bottom lip as I line myself up and push in.

She's heaven on earth. So tight and wet that the feeling of her body erases every thought from my mind. I stop worrying about the blood and the alley. I stop worrying about where I was beforehand and how I got there.

All that exists is the sensation of her hot core around me. She rocks her hips and moans, long and low, her pussy clenching around me as she comes.

Then she lets go and rides me, crying out as she comes again. I thrust into her faster, deeper, the heat between us getting stronger until I'm inhaling her moans and exhaling grunts.

"Come inside me," she begs. "Dean, I need to feel it."

She gasps as I start to come, balancing against me so I'm buried as deep as I can be. The pulses are blindingly good and steal my breath as I pump myself inside her, letting my body take control.

Fuck. I lose control and come buried deep inside of her.

I pant against her neck, breathing in the scent of her skin while she runs her fingers through my hair.

"I love you," she whispers. More heat swells through my body. "I love you. I know it's so hard, but don't forget, okay? I need you to remember."

"I will," I promise, even though I know it's not a promise I can keep. "I could never forget you."

CHAPTER 11

HALEY

Ever since I was a kid, I liked to listen to the local news. Half-listen, really, since I don't pay full attention to whatever they're saying. In the evenings they run out of crime stories pretty early on and move to human interest pieces. Last week I saw one about a woman who was turning a hundred years old and had lived in the same house for over half a century. Tonight, they're interviewing a man who lost his house in a fire and ended up buying a food truck. Now he drives around to different towns and sells people lunch after the local farmer's market.

Maybe I'm a busy body, maybe I just want to know how much bad there is compared to how much good. I'm not sure.

I take a sip of my wine, cuddled up on my sofa, and scroll

on my phone. I'm not really paying attention to the online shopping I'm doing, either. New art for my office, maybe. The abstract piece I've had in there could use a change. There are hundreds of prints to choose from.

A landscape could be good.

This is a habit of mine I'm aware has its pros and cons. Mindlessly scrolling, half paying attention, unwinding with a glass of wine and then I sleep, deeply and soundly.

I flip through different prints of the countryside on some art site that came up as an ad. A painting of a lake catches my eye. Oh—the artist has done a ton of different paintings at all times throughout the day and night.

The sound from the food truck segment cuts off as I take another sip of my wine.

"We're interrupting our previous segment to bring you breaking news." There's a tension in the anchor's voice that isn't usually there. My body stills. I've never seen this particular anchor get shaken up over anything, but now she stares into the camera like she's trying to hide her shock. "The body of a man was discovered early this morning by members of the local police department. Darell Hunt was found—"

Darell Hunt. They flash his picture up on the screen. It's a headshot taken at his most recent job—not the school I went to, but a different private school. He still looks the same in the photo. Perfectly recognizable. He aged around his eyes and has more gray to his hair... but when I look at him, the memory of what he used to be is all that I see.

My body stills, the trauma taking hold and I have to remind myself I'm not there, he has no control over me. In fact, the bastard is dead.

Footage of an alley with yellow police tape across the entrance flashes on the screen as the anchor recaps how a call came in from a concerned citizen. By then, Mr. Hunt, a husband and uncle to three children, had been dead for hours, his body found early in the morning.

I swallow thickly, my heart racing. And the flash of who I thought I saw yesterday outside of my office comes to mind. *Thump, thump*, it's hard to hear over the pounding in my chest.

The broadcast cuts to a press conference led by the local police chief.

He looks down at his notes, blinking in the bright lights. "We're prepared to announce to the public that several recent homicides appear to be connected. The manner of death—"

Thump, thump, thump. I cling to the glass of wine, not daring to take my eyes off the screen.

Lots of cameras flash. People shout questions. The police chief repeats several times that he can't give out certain details of an active investigation.

"One more question." He points into the crowd of reporters.

"Thank you, sir," a man calls from the reporters off-camera. "Does the police department have reason to believe that these homicides might have been committed by the same individual? In other words, are we looking for a serial killer?"

Chills run down my spine and panic runs through me.

"That's certainly a possibility," the police chief answers.

It cuts back to the anchor, who's joined by her co-host, and they immediately pick up the thread. People must have been working at top speed behind the scenes at the station, because nobody suggests going back to the segment about the food truck.

Serial killers are guaranteed to get more attention after all. Pictures of famous serial killers in history flash up on the screen. The anchors compare the local homicides—the information they have, anyway—and discuss things the public can do.

"Keep your doors locked," the first anchor says. "If you see suspicious activity near your home, please call and report it. Staying vigilant is the best way to stay safe."

"The best thing we can do," her co-host says, "is to stay alert. Have the police informed the public of any connections between the victims?"

"Not as of this broadcast, no. That information would certainly represent a turning point in the investigation. Even if no suspects have been taken into custody, a solid connection between the victims would point law enforcement in the direction of—"

They keep posing questions to each other, reading and re-reading the statement from the police department. All the while, I sit perfectly still, unable to move and I don't know if it's the previous learned condition from being in that hellish place, or if it's simply shock.

A *serial* killer.

My chest is tight and cold, and so are my fingers.

By then, the news anchors have decided that there's definitely a serial killer on the loose. They're predicting that the police will confirm that within the next few days.

"It's only a matter of time," the anchor says. She's settled into the story now and doesn't seem to be affected. Her professional mask is on. "With similarities of this kind, it seems unlikely that this would be the work of many different individuals, or individuals from different groups. Now, the police haven't said as much, but it's possible the bodies were discovered with evidence that would reveal the motive."

"We'll have more on that at ten," her co-host says into the camera, his smile wide, and the broadcast goes to commercial.

A car dealership commercial blares from the screen, and I grab for the remote to turn down the TV.

Panic races through me and I have to close my eyes and focus on my breathing.

If one glass of wine didn't work, I should have another one. I get up automatically and refill my glass, then stop at my front windows. I peek out the gap between the curtains.

As if he'll be there. As if he knows I'm thinking of him.

There's nobody in front of my house. I didn't think there would be, but my empty yard is a relief. I tug the curtains shut tight so that there's no gap at all. Nobody can look in on me now.

Then—although I know I locked it earlier—I double-check all the locks. They're all exactly how I left them. My house is safe and sound.

I sip my wine, making a point to savor it as I go back to the living room. The commercial break is still going. A movie trailer plays on the screen, the explosions almost too quiet to hear.

I've just sat back down on the couch and pulled a blanket over my lap when my phone rings.

It's a blocked number.

I hesitate, hovering my thumb over the button to decline the call. It's a fifty-fifty chance with calls like these. Sometimes, patients call me from blocked numbers, and I want to be available to them whenever I can.

Other times...

I hit the button to accept the call.

"Hello?"

"I saw the news."

My mother's voice doesn't make adrenaline spike in my body anymore. It did for a long time. Now it's the opposite. When I hear her speak, I get extremely calm and still.

"Mother," I answer and I can't hide the chill in my tone.

I know that's a protective response. That's my body reacting to the trauma of my past. I want to be ready for anything she might say or do, so all my senses prepare to take in every word.

"The news, Haley. Have you been watching?"

I take a deep breath, even though I know she's waiting for me to respond. I can choose to do that however I want. I can hang up the phone, if I want. I can refuse to answer. But that feels like running away without addressing the problem, and I don't want to do that.

"I've asked you to leave me alone," I tell her, as calmly as I can. "If you call me again, I'll have the protective order enforced. I'll go to the judge and tell them you violated it. You know the terms."

My mom scoffs. There's a small shake in her voice. "That restraining order is bullshit and you know it, Haley."

"It's not bullshit, and you know that, too. We've had this conversation before, and I'm getting tired of having to repeat it over and over again."

"I want to help." Her voice quavers even more. "I want to help you, Haley. I want to be there for you."

"That's not an option for you."

"But it should be. I've apologized. I've told you so many times that I didn't—"

"And I've told you that I don't want to hear from you. You can help me by leaving me alone. If you really care about what I want, you'll stop violating the restraining order."

"That order isn't right." Her tone turns pleading and defeated, like she really thought I'd change my mind this time. There's no doubt in my mind that my mom watched the same news broadcast I just did. I don't know how it made her think she should call me. "It kills me that I can't be there for you when—"

"When what, Mom? There's nothing to help me with. You watched whatever you watched, and I'm still not interested in having any contact with you. I'll never want to have contact with you again. That's because of what you did."

"Haley—"

"You can't go back and change what you've done, and I can't change what I went through and how you didn't believe me. How you tried to send me back! Now I'm choosing to move forward with my life. That means moving forward without you. That's my decision, and it's final."

"I saw that man outside your office," her voice cuts through, as if she didn't hear what I said. She never hears me. She never has.

"Why were you at my office?" I question although a voice at the back of my head is screaming, *what man?*

My heart races and I have to stand up, I have to move. I can't sit still any longer.

"Because I wanted to see you. And your boyfriend, don't think I don't know," she adds.

"Are you stalking me?" I question, my voice hitching.

"You should stay away from him, Haley. He's no good! A mother knows."

No good? My heart drops. *A mother knows?*

"You know nothing and you don't listen. You need to stop!" I tell her and my throat tightens at the last word. Tears prick my eyes. "You're the one who said I was rotten, let me be by myself and leave me alone.

"But, Haley..." Her breath hitches on the other end of the line. I feel nothing in response. When I was a kid, I would have felt guilty for making her cry. I would have been desperate to help her feel better. Now I don't feel any of that empathy, at least for her. If she wanted me to feel empathy towards her, she should have given some to me when I needed it most. "I love you. I'm your mother, and I—"

"Don't contact me again, or I'll go to the judge. I'm not giving you any more chances."

I hang up and drop my phone into my lap. It disappears into a fold in the blanket. My chest heaves as I try to steady my breath.

She loves me how she knows how. That part of these conversations—which I never want to have with my mother—is what makes me the most exhausted. My mother claims to love me, but she won't listen to what I say. All it means is that she feels like I owe her a relationship.

I feel a flicker of hurt. I'm a little sorry for my mother. Not enough to ever want to speak to her again, but sorry that they got sucked in by those people at that school. My father left when I came back, and she was all I had. And I was all she had in many ways too.

The sorry feeling only lasts for a minute or two. Yes, my mother was lied to, but they also had to be the kind of people who would accept those lies. She never looked deeper into what happened at those kinds of places.

They called it a school, and men showed up in the middle of the night to arrest me. What kind of person lets that happen? What kind of mother hides in her bedroom and lets her daughter get dragged out of the house?

My mother, that's who.

No. I'm never going to want to speak to her again. I've done a lot of work to be satisfied with my life, and she bears some of the responsibility for why that was so hard, and why I suffered so much in the process.

Then she didn't believe me. She tried to send me right back to them. She called me insane. I fucking hate her. I hate what she did to me. What she made me.

I'm done with her. I'm done with my parents. One more phone call, and I *will* go to the judge.

As if fate heard my thoughts, my phone rings again.

I fish it out from the blankets, ready to unload on a woman who won't hear a word of it. Just for the sake of hearing myself scream.

This time, the number isn't blocked. I can see exactly who it is. I'm quick to answer.

"Hi. How are you?"

There's some noise on the other end of the line, like he's outside in the breeze. The rustling continues for a few seconds, then clears.

"Haley."

My heart kicks up, pushing past my calm. The sound of his voice always does this to me. Aden's voice isn't something I can teach myself to respond to, not that I'd want to. I can only react on a deep level.

"Did you see?" I ask him, "The news that was just on?"

He's quiet on the other end of the phone.

"Aden." I pull the blanket tighter to my body, relishing the warmth. It would be warmer if his arms were around me. "I'm here. Are you alright? Tell me if you're okay."

I wait, listening to him breathe. I can tell he's deciding what to say. The wind blows a little louder, then quiets down again. I push the blanket off and get to my feet. The waiting is easier if I move around a little bit.

I wander across the living room to a low bookshelf and run my fingers over the spines. There are mostly textbooks here, but also a few novels and one other book.

Sometimes he needs time to think of what to say. He needs a moment of just knowing I'm there. I get that. More than anything, I get that we need a moment sometimes to understand what's going on in our heads.

I pull that book off of the shelf, carry it back to the couch, and set it on the coffee table. Then I trace the cover with my fingertips, focusing on the shape.

Down, and over. Down and over. The shape never changes. The lines of the book are always the same. The edges of the cover are getting a little worn from how many times I've done this, but that's okay.

They won't break completely, just like I didn't break completely. Lots of people tried, but they couldn't do it. Like my mother. I almost tell Aden but I bite my tongue.

I survived. I got out. We both got out. I have all the patience Aden needs. For him, and for me. For both of us together.

Down, and over. Down, and over. I trace the corners with my eyes closed.

"Can you—" I can hear him exhale, as if he doesn't want to ask this of me, but can't keep the words inside. "Can you come out tonight?"

"I don't know about tonight. I—"

I open my eyes, then open the book. The page I flip to is worn down a little, too, because I always flip to this page.

It's the page with Dean's picture. I don't know why I pulled this book out. I wasn't thinking of it. I was thinking of what seeing him like that would do to me.

I remember when he looked like he does in this picture.

I remember everything about him when this photo was taken.

"I don't know," I say softly. "I don't know."

CHAPTER 12

DEAN

10 YEARS AGO

Today is like any other day at this place. The shuffling of feet is vaguely heard in the background of the lunch hall, as is the slow drip of a leaking pipe.

The school. The prison. It doesn't matter what it's called. No names matter to me anymore.

The only person's name that matters is the one belonging to that girl.

I still don't have her name.

I listen whenever I can, hoping one of the teachers or staff members will let it slip. They talk about everyone in here the same way, without using many descriptions, so I've heard a few names. I'm not sure if any of them belong to her.

If I knew what her name was, I wouldn't say it out loud. I'd keep it safe and protected. I definitely wouldn't call to her even though I want to. That would be breaking every rule in this place, and I'd probably end up buried under the floorboards.

They'd never let me hear the end of that one. All the bastards here would want to know how I learned her name in the first place. They hate it when we know each other from outside.

Nothing scares these people, but I guess the thought of us finding each other and comparing notes in the outside world makes them a little nervous.

If I knew her name, the most I would do is whisper it under my breath when everybody else was asleep. Just to hear how it sounds coming from my lips.

I want to know the shape of it in my mouth.

I want to know how it feels to say her name. I wish she'd say mine too. I want her to know it. I wonder if she'd call out to me. I wish she would. I'd do anything for her to say my name.

That's what I'm thinking about in the lunchroom, pushing around the chunks of boiled chicken in rice with the plastic spoon. Nothing about the way the day has gone so far makes me think that anything will change.

The monotony of it all is enough to make you go insane.

There are always the usual things. The bastards in charge

could flip our schedule upside down. They could come up with new sick-fuck punishments to try out on us. A few of them might be in a worse mood than usual.

I guess the opposite is true, too. A few of the staff members might be in a better mood than usual. They might be extra motivated to whip us into shape. They might go above and beyond and beat us harder than we've ever been beaten. It's to beat the demons out of us, at least that's what they say.

I don't know what they get for that.

I hope it's stacks of gold or the lives of their families or something like that. I wouldn't do this for all the money in the world, unless I could use that money to burn this place down.

I let my eyes hover over the lukewarm meal, avoiding eye contact with everyone and moving as slowly as I can without getting in trouble for blocking traffic.

That's the key. If I pay too much attention to what's happening here, I get so angry I could explode. That's happened enough times for me to know that it won't get me anywhere.

If I pay too little attention, that's basically an invitation for Mr. Jay to fuck with my hands.

He loves going after my hands—loves it more than anything else. I think that's because he knows I'll need my hands to do any kind of job when I get out of here. God knows I won't be able to get a job with any kind of smarts. I've never been the sharpest knife so to speak. If he takes my hands, he'll take my entire future, if I even have one.

That makes them an obvious target. A good target and an easy one too. And he always goes for the good targets.

Beside me on the bench is another kid who sleeps in my dorm. In my periphery I recognize him. We're close enough together that I could nudge him with my elbow. I can feel the warmth of him in the air between us. But we might as well be on different sides of the country.

I don't nudge him. I don't even look in his direction.

He doesn't look at me.

One of the staff members says something to him. I don't catch what it is.

"Yes, sir," he answers, his voice flat and toneless. I think he's here about as much as I'm here. Maybe that means we'll both make it out.

Maybe it doesn't. I don't know.

I focus on putting food in my mouth. The roll is stale, and I have to wash it down with half of my water. There's some kind of vegetable. Green beans, maybe, but they're shiny with oil or something. It's not butter. I try not to pay attention to that, either.

I eat fast enough to avoid getting punished for eating slowly, and slowly enough to avoid getting punished for eating too fast.

When my food is gone, I fold my hands in my lap and stare at the table. That's the safest place to look. Can't meet anyone's eyes with my head down.

I sit up straight.

I think about the girl.

I think about her face in the room with no cameras, and I think about her face on the other side of that glass.

I'm not paying much attention at all to the lunchroom, which is why I almost miss it when the riot starts.

It starts because of Mr. Jay.

One minute, I'm sitting still, waiting to be dismissed.

The next minute, there's a sound.

It's the sound of a hand hitting skin. More specifically, the sound of a palm slapping someone's face. Hard.

I don't look up because of the slap. People get hit all the time here, and rule number one is that we're never supposed to look at anyone else.

But then there's another sound.

Normally, the only sound after somebody gets hit is an involuntary grunt or a cry or a gasp if the person is new.

The second sound is a growl.

That's the sound of somebody snapping. Of somebody deciding that they've had enough.

That hasn't happened in a while and I wonder if it's someone new here. Someone who doesn't know any better.

I pick my head up and look before I can think about the rules.

I see the kid immediately. He's one of the guys from my dorm. I usually don't hear a single word out of him. I can't remember the last time I heard him talk, if I ever heard him talk. The growl he let out might be the first time I've ever heard his voice.

I do know his name, though. I've seen him respond to it a time or two.

But never anything like this.

He puts both hands on the table with a hard slap in front of him and gets to his feet.

The room is dead silent. Nobody moves. Nobody even breathes. I don't hear a single piece of cutlery hitting a single plastic tray. Without looking around, I know that everybody's eyes are on him, just like mine.

He's fully out of his seat when Mr. Jay's brow furrows and we all recognize that look.

Somebody behind me takes a deep breath.

I guess we're all realizing that the kid has a couple of inches on Mr. Jay.

He stares at Mr. Jay's face with his lip curled, so disgusted that his cheeks are red.

The whole world seems to stop at this moment. If somebody told me that the whole planet paused to find out what would happen between some kid and Mr. Jay, I would believe it.

Then the kid's hands come up. I can practically feel everybody's heads move just a little to follow his fists. It seems surreal, like a game on TV. I haven't seen one of those since I came here.

Unlike the boxing matches my dad used to watch, there's so much anger. So much thick tension that suffocates the room.

The crack of Mr. Jay's jaw ricochets off the wall.

An energy goes through the room. That's everybody understanding, all at the same time, that we outnumber the staff in the lunchroom. That they aren't the most powerful. That they can be broken too.

Everything had been so routine and so calm that Mr. Jay only has one other guy in here with him.

There are a lot more of us than there are of them.

Mr. Jay's eyes get wide, like he's just realized that he's outnumbered at the same time as the rest of us. Although he strikes back, he misses.

That's when the kid takes the second swing.

Mr. Jay isn't ready for it. He blinks like he thinks he might've lost his mind—there's no way this can be happening to him—and doesn't pull away in time.

The hit lands hard and snaps Mr. Jay's head around.

It all happens so fast. Like a blur in a single breath.

Before he's recovered, the kid barks, "Stand up straight!" and hits him again, tears in his eyes. He screams and I can't help but to get to my feet. Like the other kids.

The guy next to me yells out, "It's time for your punishment."

The noise is incredible. The staff here yells all the time to the point that I barely notice their voices anymore.

The sound of everybody yelling is a rush of adrenaline all on its own. It courses through me, and I feel like I could do anything. I could tear down the walls with my bare hands. I could fly. I could spit fire.

Anything.

But there's only one thing I truly want. Even in the madness and chaos. I want to find her. I want to find the girl. I want to know her name and keep it with me forever.

But I'm too swept up in the momentum of what's happening in the lunchroom. It's not a fight anymore. It's a full-blown riot.

Tables being turned over, kids on top of them screaming. Someone pulls the fire alarm.

It happened too fast. And I'm standing in the center of what feels like the world burning.

A bunch of guys surge around Mr. Jay, fists flying, and they pull away just as fast. I can't see him when they do. He must be on the ground. Hitting him must have lost its appeal. I can't see how, but then somebody grabs my elbow and pulls.

This is our chance to run away. This is our only chance. It's chaos, and we might be able to take advantage of it.

We run for the lunchroom door and keep running. I don't know who's in charge. Maybe it's none of us. Somebody might shout something, but it's too loud to hear if anyone's giving instructions.

I don't need them, anyway. Out. Get out. That's all I need to do.

But where is she? I can't leave without her.

There's a crowd in the narrow hallway. Some of the girls are out there, too. I don't see her, but she has to be with us. I can't go against the current of all these people myself.

It's too loud to hear myself think. Staff members are shouting. More punches are being thrown. They can't get all of us. There are too many of us. We're going to get out.

I hit the fresh air and follow the kid in front of me.

We run and run and run.

I have no idea where we're going.

The riot starts because of Mr. Jay, but it ends because of the cops.

The sirens wail in the distance.

"The cops!" one kid screams out and runs the other way. Some kids run towards the cops, waving them down.

I search the crowd, even though I'm one of the first ones out, I can't leave without her.

The cops come out of nowhere. The first thing I see is flashing lights, and then there are cars in every direction. A few kids split off and sprint away from the road. I trip over another kid and end up on the ground in the middle of the road. In shock, I watch as they pile out of so many cars. A dozen... maybe more.

They scream at us. They pull out guns at us. The voices

all seem to meld together.

1 forgot, for a small fraction of time, 1 forgot we were the bad ones. A cop puts his foot in the middle of my back and pins me there while he cuffs me.

"Fuck," 1 whisper. Yelling will make this worse, but *fuck*. We were so close. 1 cry out that they need to help us. Fuck, 1 beg them to help us. But there is no help for kids like me.

Before 1 can think right, I'm shoved into the back of a cop car with three other guys. The drive to the nearest police station isn't as far as 1 thought it would be. That's the most disappointing thing of all. 1 thought we were in the middle of nowhere this entire fucking time and had no chance to get to anyone who could help, and it turns out they were *right fucking there.*

"Call the parents," one of the cops shouts over the noise inside the car. Some of the other kids are trying to explain. They're begging. *Begging.* 1 don't say anything. "We need to get in contact with the parents here."

My dad. Please for fuck sake, let me talk to my dad.

"That won't happen," the officer behind the desk says. "Protocol is to send them back. You're in the custody of the program."

What the fuck? They have a protocol for if kids escape that hellhole?

It's then the stench of fear fills the cabin of the parked police car.

"You'll stay here until we have eyes on all of the minors. We'll charge the ones who started it with assault," the cop tells us, pointedly looking into our eyes. "Was it one of you little shits?" he asks and I've never felt hopelessness like I do now.

The other kids scream out what they're doing. The kid on the far right won't stop crying. And I sit there, knowing what waits when we get back. I could fucking throw up.

"I think we need to call the parents," the first cop argues, standing outside the car. It's too fucking hot back here, I need to get out. I need out of here.

"The school will contact their guardians. We need to get them back."

"Please," one of the kids shouts. "Contact our parents, please! Let me talk to them!"

"Protocol," the cop who's seemingly in charge says. "We have to release you to your custodians."

The kid to my left, the one who's been blabbing says he's got to throw up.

At least they let him out for that.

Fuck... I need to find a way out. We've got to get the hell away from this place and hide. I'll hide forever to never have to go back.

CHAPTER 13

HALEY

With barely any sleep and a long day in the office where my mind wandered too much and focus was hard to come by, I come through my front door with my head fuzzy and my body exhausted. I didn't sleep well last night after the call from my mom. I swear the stairs creaked and floors groaned all night, like the threat of someone sneaking around.

I had to remind myself, they're just the sounds my house always makes. Sometimes the floor creaks and the wind blows on the roof. There was nobody there.

Even if something inside of me refused to believe that. Even if my pulse was panicked and sleep brought me terrors. When morning came, I was just fine and there was no one else there waiting in a dark corner.

Just me.

Focusing on my patients was tough today and took a ton of my mental energy.

I drop my keys on the table in the entryway, and—

A sound. From the kitchen.

I freeze in place, my blood icy with fear. I try to breathe past it, but my heartbeat is all off. How fast can I get out? If I move backward toward the door, I could try, but I'd have to unlock it, and that would make a sound, and—

Aden comes out into the hallway, his hands up.

Fucking hell. My tense body relaxes and all the air rushes out of me. "Aden. God. I—I just thought—"

I rub my tired eyes rather than finish the sentences.

He comes toward me slowly, like he doesn't want to scare me any more, and wraps me up in his arms. "I'm sorry. I didn't mean to scare you." There's a smirk on his lips like this is funny. But he doesn't know...

"I thought you were my mom," I breathe the excuse against his chest.

"Shh." He strokes my hair and holds me closer. "You know she can't hurt you anymore."

I do. I know that. I know I can choose how to respond to this situation. I burrow into Aden's chest and breathe. He smells warm and clean, and I need every bit of comfort he can offer. I cling to him and I love how he holds me back. I needed this.

As he rubs soothing circles on my back he seems to realize how shaken I really am. "She can't do anything to you anymore," he reassures me.

"I know," I finally manage to say. "I know she can't." Repeating the words out loud always helps. "But she called."

Aden's hand stops on the back of my head, his fingers in my hair. "What? What did she say?"

"Oh, God. It was nothing new. She said the same things as always. She wants to be there for me. She thinks she should be able to support me. As if she could ever understand how to do that."

My chest aches in a tightening way.

He makes a soft sound, and his hand starts moving on my hair again. "You okay?"

"Not really." I let out a final deep breath, wanting to release all that's come over me.

"Yeah. I could tell something was going on."

"I'm sorry."

"Don't be sorry. None of that is your fault. I could tell, is all. I was worried about you, so I came here to check on you. Should've told you beforehand. I won't scare you again." He smiles down at me before kissing the tip of my nose. "Promise," he adds and with his handsome smile I have to smile back up at him.

"It's okay." I curl my fingers into the back of his T-shirt.

"It's okay. I'm glad you're here. I need you."

Heat flares up everywhere inside me. It melts through my fear and my anxiety, and then my body realizes that Aden is here. He's here with me, and nobody can take him away.

Knowing I can have him—that I do have him—sends a heavier wave of heat between my legs. He's been my cure to all I went through. The balm to everything broken inside of me.

That simple comfort is my therapy. My drug. My everything.

Aden puts his hand under my chin and tips my face to his.

I kiss him harder than I meant to, but I can't stop. I'm hungry for him. I've wanted him all day. All of last night, too, and I can't wait anymore.

He walks me backward until I'm against the wall and keeps kissing me, deeper and deeper until I've fully melted against the wall and into him.

"Haley," he says, voice rough. "Yeah, that's it. You don't have to worry anymore. I've got you. I'm here."

I part my lips for another kiss, and he gives it to me.

By the time he pulls away to catch his breath, all the stress of the day has melted off me. All I want is Aden. I want him to touch me everywhere, and I never want him to leave.

Our eyes meet for a few long seconds. I know he's thinking the same thing I am.

Nobody can stop us.

Nobody can make us look away, or punish us for looking.

He puts his hand to my chin again, softer this time, and holds my face still.

And then he just stares, his cheeks flushed from how he kissed me and his lips wet. His eyes roam over my face, drinking me in, and my heart twists with a warm ache. I wish this didn't mean so much to me. I wish I'd never gone to that school.

But it means everything to me, just like Aden. I can accept that it happened to me because I have to accept it. I'll never appreciate it. I'll never be grateful to anyone at that school.

The one thing I'm grateful for is Aden.

I'm grateful to him for surviving. I'm grateful to myself for doing the same.

He comes in for another kiss, slower and gentler but just as hot. I taste him once, then twice, and then we're all over each other again, pulling at each other's clothes.

Aden picks me up. I sling my legs over his hips and wrap my arms around his shoulders and kiss him like I'll never get to kiss him again while he walks us to my bedroom.

Then he strips my shirt over my head and pushes the rest of my clothes down and off. I run my fingertips over his bare skin. He has scars underneath his shirt. Some of them are from school. Others happened after. I kiss them one by one, caressing them, and drag my hands lower until I wrap my hand around his hard length.

He groans, his head dropping back, and lets me stroke

him a few times, working the droplet of precum from his tip over the head.

He's so fucking hot.

With a firm possessive grip, he puts his hands on my waist and pushes me onto the bed.

Aden crawls over me, pushes my knees to my chest, and holds them there while he devours me. His tongue laves over every inch of my pussy. He licks me like he'll die if he can't keep tasting me, stroking the tip of his tongue into my entrance, then finally working his way up to my clit.

I don't know how many times I come with my hands in his hair. I just keep pulling him in and in and in, and he keeps working at my clit until I'm oversensitive and gasping.

"Aden," I say, pushing his head away from my thighs. "Aden. Just—just a minute. I can't—I can't—"

"Mmm. Can't you?" He keeps one hand on my thigh and slides two fingers into me, sliding them in and out at a slow pace. I clench down around them, so he buries them deeper and finds my G-spot.

"Oh, God, Aden, Aden. That's so—oh, God."

It's so much pleasure, and Aden shows no signs that he's willing to stop. It builds deep inside me, expanding around my hips and curling up in my belly. I don't exist anymore. I couldn't put a thought together if I tried. I'm made of nerve endings and Aden's hand on my thigh. His touch is all that matters in the world.

He adds a third finger and I arch up into it, making sounds I can't stop.

"Fuck, you're beautiful like this." He sounds awed, almost as if this is the first time we've been together this way. It isn't, but it warms me up all over again that he still feels for me like that. "I could never get tired of this. If I could make you come on my fingers for the rest of my life, I'd do it. I don't think I'd ever stop."

"You'd keep me in bed with you forever?"

"Longer than forever." His fingers stroke my G-spot as his thumb finds my clit. He's so gentle that I moan out loud and relax into the touch.

With my eyes closed, I can't see him smiling, but I can hear it in his voice. "Yeah, you like that. You're so fucking wet. Are you ready to take my cock yet, or should I make you wait a little longer?"

"Don't," I whine, my breath hitching. "Don't make me wait. I've wanted you all day. I've been so patient, and I don't—" He curls his fingers. "Aden, I can't wait. Please don't make me wait. I need you." How often do I tell him that? Far too much I think. It's then I think of Dean, but the thought comes quickly and then leaves.

"Alright baby." He moves over me and leans in for a kiss. I can taste myself on him, and he lets me until he uses both of his hands to turn me over, slow and gentle. Aden pulls my hips up in the air just as gently.

I wriggle my ass side to side. I feel empty without him, needy and wanting.

"Fuck me hard," I beg, pushing my face into the pillows. "Please," I beg.

"I will," he promises, his hands sliding over my hips. He notches himself at my opening, his fingers flexing, and then thrusts in.

He fills me to the hilt. I gasp at the feeling of stretching around him, of making room in my body for him. It always feels new and forbidden. I think I'll always feel like I'm getting away with something I shouldn't have.

"You can have me." Aden leans over me and kisses my nape, rolling his hips. It hits the perfect spot inside me. I curl my toes into the blanket and meet his thrusts, grinding back on him.

Aden sits up and fucks me harder. He's so deep inside me that I can't open my eyes. I grab the pillows for dear life with one hand and reach between my legs with the other.

"Yeah, fuck yeah, take it baby," he pants. "Fuck. Make yourself come on my cock. You're so—fuck, fuck, you're tight. You feel so fucking good."

My clit is so sensitive that it can only handle the gentlest touch. I circle it softly while Aden fucks me. The contrast between the force of his thrusts and the whisper-soft pressure of my fingers builds an impossible tension between my legs. That tension becomes a pleasure so thick that I almost feel drunk on it. I keep rubbing until another orgasm hits me like a wave.

Aden curses behind me, burying himself deep while I ride it out. It feels endless, my body clenching around him again and again, and I haven't begun to come down yet when his hips hitch and he starts stroking into me fast and hard.

"Gonna come," he says. "Fuck. Fuck. Gonna come."

He does, his release is hot inside me and I feel every pulse of his cock.

I don't think it's fully ended yet when he pulls out.

"Aden," I cry. "Aden, please—"

He turns me over onto my back and makes sure my head is nestled in the pillows, then crawls over me and pushes himself inside. Still hard and wanting more.

"Too much?" he murmurs into my ear.

"No. No. Could never be too much."

It couldn't. Not with his strong body over mine. Not with his arms around me. Not with my arms around him.

I'm almost delirious with pleasure, but I shut my eyes and move with him.

He's slow the second time around, taking his time with every thrust. I think he wants to fuck all night, and I wouldn't mind it. I could fall asleep like this and wake up with him still inside me.

Aden starts dropping kisses to my face and my forehead and my jaw after a while. He kisses me as slowly and deliberately as he fucks me.

This is what it's like to be able to touch someone.

This is why I survived.

Because I needed to be consumed by a man this way.

Not just any man. By Aden. I need to have him over me, exploring me, so deep inside me that I can't tell where he ends and I begin. It's all feeling between us, all heat and emotion and moment, and it makes me feel like I can breathe.

Every part of my body that had been stressed or tense from the day melts into the bed. I lift my face up for more of his kisses. Each one feels like a promise. He'll be here for me. He'll do whatever I need from him.

We made it.

We made it, and we'll never have to go back to those days.

This is our life now. This is the life we've made, and I'm going to live every minute of it with as much pleasure as I can.

It's been a long time when he shudders out another orgasm, his mouth open on my neck.

"Good?" I ask, half-asleep. I don't think I can stay awake anymore. It will feel so good to sleep and dream next to him. "Are you okay?"

"Yeah," he says, but there's something in his voice that makes me think it's not entirely true.

But I don't ask... and instead my mind wanders back to Dean.

CHAPTER 14

DEAN

When the police car pulls up in front of my house, my first thought is to run. My heart pounds and I know I've been reckless and in the back of my mind I know it's going to end with bloodshed or prison.

I've always known that's what I'm destined for.

The cops aren't going to help. I've known that since I was in school. Even if a bunch of kids show up at the station and beg for help, they'll refuse.

I'm not a kid anymore and I'm not the one who needs saving.

My head pounds and I can barely remember last night. Time blurs and all I know is the pain and flashes of what must have been.

If they wouldn't help me then, they sure as hell won't be

on my side now.

I don't run as I let the blinds go. They close and I wait.

I don't want to give them any reason to run after me. My heart races, adrenaline forced through my veins.

The lights on the car flash silently, lighting the whole street in blue and red.

They wait and wait and all the while I wait too, getting more and more anxious. Wondering what exactly they found that brought them here.

The lights go off.

Two cops climb out of the car in the dark of the street, talking to one another. They look around my neighborhood.

I swallow my defensiveness. I didn't do anything wrong, I try to convince myself of the lie.

They come up the sidewalk slowly. That's a good thing, right? If they wanted to pull something, they'd have come in fast so I didn't have a chance to get away.

I don't have to answer, I think. I debate on what to do, but fuck, part of me just wants this to end. The thought is quickly silenced by the image of *her*.

They pause in the middle of the sidewalk to talk to one another again. One of them points in the direction of the shop and the other one nods. I'm glad it's nighttime and long after I would have left the shop even if I put in extra hours. They could be coming to talk to me or question me or arrest me—whatever their plan is—in front of Rick and all the other guys if it was morning. And I don't need more people poking around or questioning shit.

I wait in the living room until they're out of sight.

A few seconds later, there's a knock at the door.

Knock, knock, knock.

They don't mention police or a warrant or anything. It's quiet. Just a knock at the door. I make myself walk slowly and calmly just like they did. When I pull the door open, a fresh breeze comes in. Night air, cooled down from the day. The kind of air I rarely felt at that place.

"Evening, officers," I say, my face mostly blank although I hope I look slightly shocked to see them. "Is there something I can help you with?" My voice is even as I glance down quickly. They each have their guns, their walkie talkies. Their uniforms are black, so it's the state not county.

My mind races and I get lightheaded so I hold on to the edge of the door.

The first one consults a notepad in his hand, then studies my face. "Evening. Are you Dean Quinell?"

"That's me," I say. I don't say anything else, just let the silence hang between us.

The two officers exchange a quick glance.

"Could we come in and talk to you for a few minutes?" the second one asks. "We have a few questions we thought you might be able to help us with."

My hand tightens even further. I know better than to let

cops inside my house, but to kick them out would probably make it seem like I had something to hide. I go against my better judgment.

"Sure." I open the door wider and step back into the entryway. "Come on in."

"Thanks," the first one says, and gives me a little nod.

They follow me into the living room. It's a normal living room. I'm a normal person. They're not going to find anything in here.

I'll invite them in, but we're not going to sit down for a long chat. I stop in the middle of my living room. "What's this about?" I ask. The cops look everything over, from the soft gray sofa to the recliner I got for my dad when he comes to visit. There are a couple of pictures here and there, one of my mother and I when I was just a babe. The TV is hung on the wall and under it a couple of plants that were gifts. Everything gets a look with quick glances from the cops, then both of them turn to me, standing up a little straighter.

"We'd like to ask you about your whereabouts on a few different dates," the second cop says, his eyes on mine. Now he's watching to see what I'll do.

The first cop clears his throat, then flips to another page in his notebook. "On the night of—"

He goes through a few different dates. A few different nights, really. I listen to his list, blank-faced. That's the only thing the school ever taught me.

When he's finished with his list, they look at me expectantly.

I shake my head. "What's this about?"

"We're investigating a series of murders in the area," the second cop says.

My brow raises and I stand a little straighter, "Murders? What do you think I know about any murders?"

The first one looks at me. "We're going through the list of children enrolled at a particular school the victims all worked at… it seems you attended Cedar Woods Academy?"

I let them see how hearing the name of that place makes me feel, which is sick. I lean back and grip the sofa and stare down a moment.

"You mean the fucked up school that got shut down? Yeah I went there, years and years ago but I don't know anything about any of the faculty or any of the other students," I lie and the temperature of my body heightens.

The second cop shuffles, one of his hands going to his belt. "I take it that means you have some resentment."

"I would be concerned about anyone who doesn't have resentment after they heard—fuck. Everyone heard what happened at that place. Who wouldn't be angry?"

"Let's go back to the list." The first cop doesn't look at his buddy. "Where were you two nights ago?"

I look at the second man instead.

"Are you asking everybody who went to that school, or—"

"Only the former students who have criminal records

right now," the first cop says, cutting me off.

Fuck. This is all so fucked.

Just when I'm about to answer—I don't even know what I'm going to say—there's a loud knock at my door. I snap my mouth shut. More cops?

"Dean?" Thank God. "Dean I know you're in there. I'm coming in, okay?"

The front door opens and my girlfriend comes in, looking as gorgeous as she always does even though it's almost ten at night. I don't know how she knew the cops were here. I don't care how she knew. I'm just glad I'm not facing this alone anymore.

"Good evening, officers." She sounds so innocent but also shocked as she stands in her cream sweater and skinny jeans. So surprised to find cops in my living room. She looks like the kind of person who's had a perfect life. Who's never seen anything horrific happen in front of her and been forced to watch. "I'm Dean's girlfriend." She comes over to me and gives my hand a quick squeeze. "I saw the car outside. Is everything okay?"

"We had some questions for Mr. Quinell and his whereabouts two nights ago."

My girlfriend answers quickly. "Oh! He was with me. We had dinner around eight, and then we went to bed around ten. He doesn't stay up late when he has work the next morning."

"Did he have work the next morning?"

"Yes, like most days." Her smile fades. "It was a normal morning. I got ready and went to work and so did Dean."

"You went to work at the repair shop next door?" Mr. Quinell the first cop asks, his voice starting to soften.

"Yeah. That's where I work." I answer as respectfully as I can.

"Will they corroborate your statement if we stop by in the morning?"

I nod, but she speaks up.

"Of course they will," my girlfriend says. "Rick will tell you Dean was the there. He doesn't miss work, you know. He's a reliable person. Rick will tell you that, too. Dean is a good man." Her voice tightens as she tells them such a lie.

The cops glance between her and I. "We'll do that, then," the second cop says finally. "A call in the morning should be fine."

"I don't really have much else to say," I tell them.

"If there's anything else you need, you'll let us know, right?" My girlfriend follows the cops to the door and holds it open for them.

They answer her. I don't catch what they say.

"Okay," she calls into the night. "Stay safe."

"Thanks for your time, Mr. Quinell."

"You're welcome." I'm reluctant to answer and I honestly don't know what they're thinking.

The door clicks shut, and I hear her flip the lock. Then she comes back into the living room, crosses to me, and puts her hands on my face, pulling me in for a soft kiss. My hands go to her waist, and I hold her tight. Maybe too tight. I need to feel her, and I can't let go.

She deepens the kiss, letting me taste her, and my pulse slowly stops racing. Damn, she tastes sweet. Sweet like the only woman I'll ever need.

With a soft sigh, she pulls back, her forehead pressed against mine.

"You lied," I breathe. I know the cops are gone and they can't hear me, but I feel like there are ears everywhere, listening for anything I might say to implicate myself.

The only person here is her. She opens her eyes, strokes her fingers through my hair, and looks seriously into my eyes as if this is the most important thing she'll ever tell me. My heart thuds. It can't take much more adrenaline, but the truth is in the air between us, and I've never felt her love so strongly before.

I've never felt any love so strongly before. I didn't know it was possible to experience this depth of feeling.

I'm alive. I'm so alive for the first time in years. Maybe decades. Those were such simple words out of her mouth, and out of mine, and yet they carry more meaning than most things I've ever said.

"Don't ever say that out loud again," she tells me beneath her breath. More simple words, but I won't. I won't ever say them again. She goes up on tiptoes for another kiss, then slides one of her hands over my chest until she can grab my hand. "Come on. Let's just watch some mindless TV and go to bed. That was enough excitement for one night, I think."

I pull her back toward me, capturing her in my arms.

"I love you." Her eyes go soft and shiny and overflowing with love. I can practically see her heart there when she looks at me. "More than you'll ever know."

We make it to the sofa, but neither of us turns on the TV. I lay her back on the cushions and push her hair out of her face and kiss her, letting my body take over.

Both of us need gentleness tonight, so I take off her clothes slowly and carefully, kissing every bit of exposed skin I find along the way. She arches underneath me, making little sounds and pulling me as close as she can. I drag my lips over so much soft skin.

I kiss down over her ribs and over the soft dip at her belly and lower, to where she's wet and eager for me already. She whines when I kiss her clit and lifts her hips to make it easier for me.

I take my time with every inch of her. The tender skin at the inside of her thighs. The curve of her calf. Between her legs. Loving her for loving me. For covering for me and cleaning up after my mess.

I crawl over her, her taste everywhere, and push myself inside her, slow and savoring every moment.

I stroke into her, emotion swelling up in my chest. I don't have to look over my shoulder anymore. I don't have to let all that pain consume me. I'm free to enjoy the pleasure of her. To give her more pleasure in return.

It's too much. How could I ever be worthy of her?

"I don't deserve you," I say into her mouth, fucking her as slow as I can so that it lasts. I want it to last.

She pushes on my shoulders and turns us over so she can ride me, running her fingers through my hair again and looking into my eyes. I think I'll always get a thrill from looking at her like this.

"You deserve more than me," she says, her voice trembling. She grinds down on me in intoxicating circles. I won't be able to hold out if she keeps this up. I'll have to fuck her again. Once isn't enough for tonight. It will never be enough. "I love you so much. There's nothing you could ever do that would make me not love you. You know that, right?"

"I know." I'm telling her the truth. After what she did for me tonight, I could never doubt her. "I know."

"I'll protect you." Her mouth meets mine for a kiss that matches the movements of our bodies. Slow. Soft. Deep. "I promise."

And then I breathe something I know I shouldn't, "I love you, Haley." I say it so low, I don't know if she hears me, but she doesn't stop her movements, and she kisses me deeply like she needs me more than ever.

CHAPTER 15

HALEY

10 YEARS AGO

He's gone.

He's gone, and I don't know what to do.

I can't think. He's gone, and that means there's nowhere for me to look for him.

He's gone, and in this place, that can only mean I'll never see him again.

The fear consumes every thought and feeling. Is my heart even beating anymore?

I stare at the open door of the room with no cameras, both hoping I'll see him and hoping I won't.

If he made it out, then I never want to see him in this place again. If he's free, then he should stay free. I know that's what he'd tell me to do. If I got away, he wouldn't want me to come back for him.

Keep running. Don't look back for anything. Never let them see your face again.

My eyes sting with tears, but I don't let them fall. I'm just so scared, and I'm not even scared for me. I'm scared for him.

He could be dead for all I know.

I've seen what they do to him. The people in charge of this place would do it. They would kill, and brush the murder under the rug. That's how they get away with everything. If they really screw up and hurt somebody too badly, they just blame it on the kid.

It makes my hands shake with rage. They can blame it on us because our parents already think we're lost causes. The teachers could tell my parents anything, and they'd eat it up. They want to be reassured that we need help beyond anything they can handle. We have to be the worst of the worst or else it's our parents who failed.

My mother is the one who sent me here in the first place because she thought I was evil. She probably still thinks I'm evil. I have no way to tell her I'm not. I don't know what she hears from the school or if they hear anything at all. They're probably just living their normal lives, hoping these kind people can get me back on the right track.

I reach down and curl my hands around the seat of the chair to keep myself from standing up and screaming.

If he was in front of me now, I'd have no problem staying still and silent for as long as it took.

I'd do anything for him. Even just to see him for a fraction of a second.

But he's not here, and I'm alone. The desire to fight is almost overwhelming.

I close my eyes for a few seconds and take deep breaths.

"Be good," I whisper to myself beneath my breath. "Play nice. Let them think you're broken."

I repeat it a few more times until I'm sure my fear is hidden. A broken person doesn't let people know who they care about because a broken person doesn't care about anyone.

"I don't care," I whisper. It's them I don't care about. I can't even lie to myself about him. I will only say that if that's what it takes to buy myself some time. Nothing I say to them means anything.

It's all fake. I'm just faking it so I can get out of here. I'm just playing the part that will lead to me getting free.

Thunk, thunk. Footsteps ricochet in the hall. I let go of the chair and fold my hands in my lap and sit up straight.

Mr. Jay comes into the room with no cameras. He doesn't try to hide how much he likes it in here. He sneers at me, his eyes roaming over my body.

I bite my tongue to stop any words from coming out of my mouth. He's a creep and a monster. If he decides to touch me, then he'll do it, and nothing I say will stop him.

He plants his feet a short distance away from my chair. If he leaned forward, he could reach me. I don't move.

Don't move a muscle, I remind myself.

Mr. Jay stares at me until my breath gets shorter. I hate waiting to find out what they'll do. It's always bad, always humiliating, and somehow I never guess right.

"Have you reflected on your actions?" he asks.

"Yes, sir." What he's really asking is whether I feel sorry for the riot. I didn't start it. While we were running, someone said something about the lunchroom. I just got swept up in it, and there was no way I was going to fight to come back to the school.

"And?" he prompts.

"And I'm sorry I broke the rules."

"You did more than break the rules. You put our school at risk."

"I'm sorry." I'm not actually sorry. I don't know how I could be. The riot felt like a dream. I was almost outside my body, going along with everybody else.

"I don't think you are."

I don't answer him. I'm playing nice. Faking it. If he expects me to argue, he'll be disappointed. I'm not going to. I just look up at him, my hands demurely in my lap.

The corner of his lip curls. He wanted me to put up a fight. The man doesn't need an excuse to hurt me, but he likes to have one, and I'm not giving it to him.

With a disgusted sigh, he jerks his head toward the door. "Get up. Follow me."

I do.

The whole school is silent except for the voices of some of the teachers. It was so loud when we were escaping. It really felt like we were about to be free. The energy was electrifying. It's the same feeling I had during those playground games when I would reach the slide that meant safety, my heart pounding and my body flooded with relief.

I'll feel that again someday. I will. I don't know how or when, or what I'll have to do to guarantee I have that feeling, but I'll get it.

No matter what.

Now, I have just have to fake it.

Mr. Jay stops at another room and gestures me inside.

I stop myself from letting out a gasp at the last second.

The room is a nightmare. Blood and dirt cover the floor, some of the mess in wide streaks, like they dragged someone who was bleeding into the room and used them to mop the concrete.

"This is your punishment."

I blink, not wanting to look at Jay. "This?"

"Clean it up."

I lift my hands in front of me. "I don't have—"

"With this."

He holds a toothbrush. Whose is this? It's been used—I

can tell that from how the bristles are sticking out. It's not mine. I thought I was used to the horrible things they did here, but my stomach clenches.

I take the toothbrush.

It's dry, not wet, so he didn't pull this out of someone's mouth.

"Get down on your knees."

I get down on my knees at the edge of the mess. "I don't have anything to—"

"Start scrubbing."

The dry toothbrush can't clean the blood and dirt off concrete but I do as I'm told. "Spit," he orders and I do. It doesn't take long for my knees to ache from my position on the floor. When I try to balance on my heels, Mr. Jay barks at me to get back on my knees.

He tells me how worthless I am. But I already knew he would say things like that. It means nothing now. His opinion is shit.

Even through my pants, my knees hurt like the skin is being cut.

Both my knees will be bruised and raw by the time he lets me out of here. That's what always happens. That's probably why there are concrete floors and no rugs anywhere. Students spend too much time on their knees. Rugs would only make that easier, and we're not here for things to be easy.

My knuckles get scraped, too. My hand is cramped around

the toothbrush when a bucket thuds down next to me.

"Keep going. And this time, use the soap."

I answer diligently, "Yes, sir."

The warm, soapy water does a better job on the filth, but all I have is a toothbrush. I don't have a mop or even a rag, so the water just gets dirty and red and collects in a pool on the floor. I tried my best to push it toward the drain with the toothbrush. The floor isn't slanted like it normally would be in a room with a drain, so I have to do it one toothbrush-sweep at a time.

I stop thinking about how long it will take. I'll be in here as long as Mr. Jay wants me to be. The floor and the mess are just his excuses. I could probably clean it until it was spotless, and he'd walk across it again with mud on his shoes just so I had to start over.

I go through the alphabet while I scrub, then count to a hundred. I try to remember science facts I learned in school. In my real school, not this one—I don't think I've ever learned anything here except cruelty.

But then I think of him. Of a different life where we're together and there's no pain.

The pain in my knees and my knuckles becomes background noise.

I swallow back tears. I had done so well keeping my mind blank, but now the thought of him blurs out the blood and dirt on the floor.

Is this his blood?

Did he lose too much to survive?

I force myself to stop thinking about things I don't know are real. I force myself to keep scrubbing. To get the room clean.

My legs hurt from my toes to my hips when I finally scrape the last bit of soap and blood and dirt into the drain. The door opens and shuts behind me. I hadn't realized I was alone. Hours must've past.

"Rinse the floor."

I stagger to my feet. My ankles were bent in an awkward position for too long, so I struggle to keep my balance. Mr. Jay points at the bucket of water. It's a deep, dirty gray color now.

The metal handle cuts into my palms when I pick it up. There's still quite a bit of water left, and I nearly fall over from the weight of it.

But I don't.

I walk a few crooked steps toward the drain, then start pouring as carefully as I can. The water streams out of the bucket and pushes the last of the mess into the drain. This floor will probably never look completely clean again, but it doesn't look like a murder scene anymore.

I did that.

I'm not proud of the job I've done—the punishment I've endured. I'm more surprised that it was possible at all. I thought the toothbrush would never get anything off that floor, even with the water.

The last of the water spills out of the bucket, and I put it down on the floor. I'm exhausted and shaking, the toothbrush still clutched in my hand. Does every room in the school look like this? Will I be scrubbing floors until I fall over dead?

It's hard to pick my head up, but I do.

Mr. Jay narrows his eyes. "Now brush your teeth."

My mouth drops open, but I close it again. I'm too numb to be shocked, but this—

"I—" My tongue is so dry that it struggles to move. "I don't have—"

"There's no need for toothpaste."

I lift the toothbrush to my mouth and push it inside. I'm not here. I'm not here, and I'm not doing this. This is happening to someone else. I'm watching it happen to someone else.

The taste is awful. I gag on it, but I know better than to think he'll let me off after a few seconds.

Mr. Jay doesn't.

He makes me open my mouth so he can be sure I've brushed every single one of my teeth with the foul toothbrush, covered in blood and dirt and soap.

When I can't stand to brush for another second, I pull it out of my mouth and bend over to spit into the drain.

"You will swallow."

I don't want to. God, I don't want to. Saliva fills my mouth. I'm going to be sick. I'm going to be sick, and then—

No. I can't.

I'm not here. This is happening to somebody else.

It's not me.

I have to fake it until I get free. I have to fake it, and that means doing whatever Mr. Jay says.

I swallow, tears pricking my eyes.

It almost comes up, but I swallow again. That happens three times before I'm certain I won't throw up. I stay bent over the drain for another few seconds, then stand up straight and face Mr. Jay. I'm a mess on the inside. I'm disgusted and afraid and tired, and I don't know how I'm supposed to keep going.

I have to keep going.

"Doesn't it feel good to do the right thing?" Mr. Jay asks in a voice that's sweet as honey. "Your mother picked this punishment for you."

"Y—" I'm almost sick again, but I choke it down. In another few seconds, I'll start crying. The only reason I make myself stop is that I'll get another punishment. I can't take another punishment. Not tonight. "Yes, sir. It feels good to do the right thing."

I keep on doing the right thing for three months before I see my mother again.

When I do, she can't believe the person I've become. She's proud of all the progress that I've made and so relieved that I finally saw how wrong I was before I came here.

My mom cries and kisses both my cheeks. "You've grown so much. You've turned out so well."

She's so pleased with everything the school has done for me that she makes me stay another two months and finish out the year so I can graduate with my classmates.

CHAPTER 16

DEAN

The next time I show up at the shop for my shift, I feel like I've been given a new lease on life. Rick gives me some mild shit over how the cops came to interview him, then slaps me on the shoulder and reminds me in a fake-stern voice to stay out of trouble.

"I always stay out of trouble," I tell him with a smirk.

"I know you do," he says with another deep laugh, his eyes twinkling. He's been in trouble when he was a kid. Thank fuck he has a soft spot for me.

What I have today is a full list of projects out ahead of me. Some of them are as simple as oil changes. There's a decent job for you. You start with dirty oil and end up with clean oil.

But mostly I fix broken things at this job. It reminds me

every time I'm here that if you really try, you can fix broken people, too.

It's not usually as simple with people. Can't swap out old parts for new ones. Can't replace dirty oil with clean. But you can take a good look at the parts that aren't working and shine them up until they do.

Mostly, anyway. At least I fucking hope you can. I don't want to be broken anymore.

"Are you going to be at the bar tonight?" Seth, another one of the guys at the shop, nudges me on his way past, a rag in his hands and his hat pushed back on his head. "I was thinking about trying that place out. I figure it must be good."

"It's just a bar. Nothing fancy."

"Yeah, but you always talk about it, and you're picky."

"Me?" I point at my chest. "You think I'm picky?"

"I think you know what you like. And you like that bar. Mind if I come along, or is it supposed to be a secret?"

"You can go wherever you want." I feel myself getting defensive, like he's trying to pry into my life, but he's right. I've mentioned my bar quite a few times at work. If I didn't want anyone to know I went there, I should've kept my mouth shut. I don't have to do that anymore. That was a school rule, not a real-life rule. I can say whatever the hell I want to whoever I want. There's only one thing I can't say, and it has nothing to do with the bar. "But I'd like to see you over there sometime. You like burgers?"

He laughs. "Who the hell doesn't like burgers?"

I shrug, "You never know."

"Yeah. I can get behind a good burger, especially when they have decent beers on tap."

"It's a bar, so they've got lots of shit on tap."

"Good." He knocks his hand against my shoulder. "I'll look for you. What time do you think you'll be there?"

I tell him what time I'm planning to head out and give him an estimate on when I'll be at my barstool. "I'm usually there at the same time most nights, so I'm easy to find."

"I know." My stomach drops. For a few seconds, it doesn't come back up. He knows I'm easy to find? What the hell else does this guy know about me? What does he think he knows? "It's okay, man. Don't look so freaked out. You live next door. Everybody knows that."

"Right."

"Right," he repeats. "You live next door, and you've never even asked us over for a game of cards."

"I didn't know you wanted to play cards."

"Where else would we play? The office?"

"You could if you wanted to."

Seth gestures around the rest of the shop. "This is work. Not everything can happen here. Haven't you ever heard of a work-life balance?"

"I don't sit at a desk all day, so no."

"I bet you have more chairs in your house." He leans in

and gives me a look. "I bet you also have a bigger fridge, which could fit more beer. And if you were really feeling friendly, you could order a pizza, and we could eat it while we played cards."

"Sounds like you're inviting yourself over."

"That's exactly what I'm doing. What do you say? Next Friday? Or do you only socialize at the bar?"

"Next Friday's fine," I tell him, mostly uneasy but at the same time, curious. I wonder if the boss put him up to this. To make me feel like I'm part of the family, as he likes to call it.

"I'll let the rest of the guys know."

I like the guys at the shop well enough—if I didn't, I wouldn't work here—but I guess I've never thought much about whether they liked me back.

I work through a complicated repair on a new-ish car—the news ones are always the worst because they have computer chips and all kinds of other bullshit built in—and then a simple repair on an old car. I take a break for lunch and go back at it, knocking two more repairs off the list.

"I'm going to make you employee of the month," Rick shouts over the whine of a drill. "Put your picture on the wall and everything."

"Hey," Seth calls from the other side of the shop. "What about me? I've been here longer."

"You're not as good," Rick answers.

"Hey, fuck you."

"Watch your mouth in my repair shop."

They both laugh at each other.

It doesn't come up again. We get a few more cars in toward the early afternoon. I let Rick know I'll stay a little later so we're not swamped in the morning. It just feels like the right thing to do, and it keeps feeling that way.

I've come pretty far.

I owe that to my girl. Even when my head is fuzzy with the other things, I know she's there for me. She's the one who keeps being there for me.

My girlfriend showed me that we don't have to stay there forever. We existed before we got sent away. We exist now. Everything that happened in the middle is just part of us. It's not all of us.

I think about that for a while I'm bent over the next car on the list.

"Hey, Aden."

I pick my head up and almost bang it on the hood, my heart in my throat. I lose sight of the engine for a few beats.

The memories are right there in front of me like they never stopped. I can feel their hands on my arms and their feet coming down on my knuckles and how almost every part of me throbbed even when I was laying in bed. I can smell the bleach in the bathrooms and the overcooked meat in the lunchroom and blood drying on my skin.

All the feelings come back, too. The heaviest despair I've ever felt. A hopelessness that went so deep I thought about dying every day. A place like Rick's shop seemed impossible to me when I was lying on a concrete floor, having my hands broken into a million pieces. A house of my own? That was never going to happen.

The torture I went through becomes one long memory that's filled with pain and screaming and worthlessness. It gets so loud that the shop fades away.

What the fuck. No one's called me Aden in years. No one but her. My Haley. My girlfriend. Only when she needs me to be Aden. When that part of me has to come out.

I didn't make it up. My friend Nathan, who I used to see all the time at the bar, is leaning in through one of the garage's doors out front. It's been fucking years since I've seen him. Since that first year I found her.

None of the other guys seem to have noticed anything happening with me. They're still going about their business.

Fuck. That was close. If it never happened again, I'd be glad.

Nathan lifts his hand. "Hey! How you doing? Saw this place was open and decided to stop by. I'm back in town. Am I interrupting?"

"No, I'm good. Good to see you man. Just let me—" I grab the nearest rag and wipe at my hands while I go across to him. It's too loud in the shop to carry on a conversation, and I need those few seconds to collect myself. My heart's going way too fast. It slows down as we step outside into the fresh air. I take my hat off and let the breeze blow through my hair. The fresh air settles me down some more. So do the sounds coming from the shop. "Next time—I don't know if you forgot, but I don't go by that name anymore."

"Oh, shit, right." He claps my shoulder. "Sorry, man. It was for therapy, right? The fuck was that called again?."

"Yeah. An anagram. I know it probably doesn't seem—"

"Nah. My fault. I won't screw it up again."

"It's fine, it's fine." I'm relieved, though. I tried to be Aden for a little while. I wanted to leave all this shit in the past. And then Haley got an idea. It was Haley's plan.

I thought people might give me shit when I started going by another name, but they didn't. They know what I went through. Honestly, they know too much.

Nathan gives me a once-over. He doesn't look concerned, exactly, but he does look...interested. Like he cares about how I'm doing. It's not because he knows what I've been doing. The plan Haley had. I have to tell myself that over and over again. People aren't looking at me because they're suspicious, or because they want to get me in trouble for looking back.

Or because they know I have that thing with my head. They don't know that part. Haley said to keep it a secret.

They're just looking.

That's what people do when they haven't had rule number one punched into them so many times it'll never leave.

"Honestly, man, I'm happy for you. The name thing seems like a decent way to—" Nathan waves his hand. "You know.

Dean, Dean, Dean. I got you man."

I let out a laugh, like it doesn't do things to me, to hear that name.

"It helps compartmentalize, you know? Keeps things separate." He changes the subject and rattles on about being back in town and needing a job. I let it all go. I leave all the thoughts that creep up to sit there and wait. Wait for Haley. She'll fix this feeling inside of me.

She always does. I'm glad she found me. I didn't know how to find her, but she was able to find me.

CHAPTER 17

HALEY

The door creaks, and all my attention focuses on the sound. My body goes so still I can feel my heart beating and hear my pulse. It's after hours at my office, so there are only a few people who could be walking in.

"Who's there?" I call, my voice steady.

"It's me."

The sound of his voice comforts me. I like knowing that the footsteps approaching belong to him. I like knowing that he came here for me, and nobody stopped him. Nobody can.

I unfold myself from my chair and get to my feet as he comes into view, the lamplight soft on his features. He knows he's not supposed to be here. We're not supposed to be seen together really, but I guess since the cops came and saw us it doesn't matter. We couldn't stay hidden forever.

"Aden?" I question. Unsure of which personality I'm talking to. Aden or Dean. His dissociative identity disorder was far too easy to diagnose when I found him. It's fucking shocking the state didn't diagnose him.

His mouth curves in a crooked smile. "Which do you want?"

"Aden," I murmur his name and kiss him, needing to stand on my tiptoes. His hands wrap around mine. The gentle side of him. The side who doesn't know all of what Dean went through. The side that doesn't remember.

I smile back at him, although my heart pounds. "Is it done?"

The smile dims a little as I wait for his response, but it doesn't fade completely. "Is what done?" he asks. Aden doesn't always know. He doesn't want to and he doesn't need to. I love them both. I need them both. Even if all of me is irreparably broken and half of him is.

"The list I gave you. The one for him. For Dean?"

"All the names are gone. Or did he add more?"

I hesitate. I always choose my words carefully with all the patients I work with, but I'm the most careful with him. He means too much to me.

I shake my head no. "If they're all crossed off, there's no reason to worry."

"Are you worried, baby?" he asks me with a sad smile.

"The news makes me worry," I admit to him and he kisses me softly before whispering at my lips, "There's no reason to worry. He's been careful. I know he has."

His eyes go soft. Part of that might be because of the light, but I know it's also because of how he feels.

He takes a breath. "You stay with me, don't you? When I'm him." Aden doesn't understand everything. But he knows how much I love Dean. I don't compare the two of them. I love them both more than anything. I need them both too.

"Always," I promise, looking him in the eye. The eyes really are the windows to the soul. That doesn't mean it's always easy to accept what you see when you look. I've seen lots of broken souls, hurting from years of abuse and losing hope that they'll ever feel normal again. "I always stay with you, both sides of you. You know I love all of you."

He squeezes my hand, a smile returning to his face. This one's brighter. "Always," he whispers.

"I love you both always." I take his other hand in mine and let out a sigh. "But I'd love to confide in Dean now if that's alright."

He lets out a quiet laugh. "Do you need to compartmentalize, Doctor?" He smirks a handsome look, but I know he wishes I didn't need Dean. I know he gets jealous. A part of me loves that. I'm selfish though. In more than one way.

He lets his eyes flutter closed for a few beats, then opens them.

"Dean?"

He doesn't smile back. "Haley," he says my name like an apology. I'm quick to kiss him. To hold him the way Aden holds me.

"You okay?" he asks me. It's the first thing he asked when he saw me. Back when I found him years ago. As if he'd been waiting years to ask me that question.

"It's been hard on me," I admit, feeling the tension in my shoulders and back. It tends to sneak up on me. "All of this. You're doing a better job than I am."

"No, I'm not." He kisses my forehead, his lips still slightly cool from the breeze outside. He smells like fresh air and cologne with a very faint undertone of oil from the shop. I also get a whiff of lemon from the soap he likes to scrub his hands with the best. "You're doing perfectly, my angel."

His mouth meets mine. I keep trying to decide which kisses I like best. Some days, all I want is something rough and biting so I can have enough sensation to forget. I want him to hurt me just a little to prove that I can handle pain—even enjoy it, if it's at the right level. Other days, all I want is soft, tender kisses.

He explores my mouth, his hands moving to cup my cheeks, thumbs running gently over my cheekbones. It feels so good to be touched like this. To be treasured above everybody else in the world. A tiny moan escapes me, and he hums back as if he could taste it, and he liked it. His teeth graze my bottom lip, not enough to hurt, and the spark of pleasure shoots down to my core.

The way I feel when I'm with him is like nothing else in the world. I could forget all my plans. Leave those in the past, too. That's what's dangerous about him. He makes me want to lock the door behind us and never come out again. I could just let him have his way with me forever.

I get lost in that fantasy for a few minutes. His touch does that to me. It makes me feel like the world could be this gentle, and my life could be this gentle, if I'd only let him take me away.

I kiss him until I have to pull back for breath. His eyes are dark with his blown pupils, and when I run my fingers through his hair he shivers in a way that's unique to him.

"It's over now," he reassures me. "It'll blow over. They'll never find out it's us."

"Not yet..." I murmur, feeling guilty. I'm the one who made the list. The one who planned it all.

"We aren't done?" he asks softly, his brow arched.

I whisper back, "There's one more."

He blinks, his hand coming to rest on my cheek. He tilts my face up another inch and holds my head still. "Who?" We wrote down every name. Every single person who laid a hand on either of us. They got their punishments that were due.

"My mother. She's snooping around and she's seen you. We can't risk her putting the pieces together. Besides, she was never punished for what she did. We have to do the right thing. We have to punish them."

He starts to pull away, but I get my hands to his neck and bring him back. "That's—"

"Dean, listen to me." I need this. I don't want to start off by saying so, but I need to be free of her interference. I need to be free of wondering if it's her when the door opens. I never want to answer my phone and hear her voice again. I've implied that to him before, but there were always other people to worry about first. And if she's watching us... she could ruin everything.

Now they're all gone. Everybody's been crossed off the list but she added her name to the fucking bottom. All she had to do was leave me alone. I would have let her live. But she couldn't do that.

There were times I thought I could let it go and just forget about her, but that's not going to be possible. She's never going to leave me alone. She'll keep trying to get back into my life until I put a stop to it.

Every person on that list deserved worse than to be killed and forgotten.

My throat closes, and I can't speak for a minute. Part of me still wishes she would change. I wish she would write to me and tell me how wrong she was for disregarding me.

I'd still want her gone, even if she did that. There are some things you can't take back.

She can never take this back. And I would do anything

for Dean. She should have never laid eyes on him. She's not worthy of judging him.

It takes a few more beats to steady myself.

I finally tell him, "She deserves it as much as the rest of them do."

He closes his eyes, his dark lashes coming to rest on his cheeks. I'll never forget how he looked the first time I saw him, back at school. The warmth I felt when his eyes met mine kept me alive for months after that. It gave me hope even when there was no reason for me to be hopeful.

Somehow, I just knew. Most people would say that you can't know so much about a person from a single glance. They're wrong. You can know everything you need to know about that person if the circumstances are just right to let you *see*.

And I *saw* him. And he saw me.

I'll always see him just how he was, and just how he is.

How both of them are.

Dean opens his eyes and strokes my hair again, centering himself. It takes a little longer this time, but finally his fingertips trace my cheekbone and down over my jaw until his hand drops to mine. He twines our fingers together. Whenever he does this, I fall for him all over again. It's his way of telling me without words that it's us against the world.

It'll always be us.

"Is this the last one?"

I step closer, still holding his hand, and kiss him.

"I promise." Another kiss. I'm sealing my promises with them. They were forbidden for so long, and now that they're not, I'll give them whenever I can. "And then we'll get the happily ever after we should have had."

"Okay," he whispers, and presses a final kiss to my forehead. "Did you write me a note?"

I take out my notebook. The time and location are already there on the page. I tear it out, fold it up, and hand it to him. "Leave it in your pocket until he's ready."

"I always do." He traces the note with the pad of his thumb, then slips it into his pocket. His eyes come back to mine with another question. "You won't leave me, right?"

"I would never leave you. I love you both."

He looks away. It's my turn to put my hands on his face so he'll look at me. I'll never be able to erase the pain those people caused, but I can do my best to make sure he doesn't feel like I'll cause him more.

"We've talked about this," I say gently. "You're both worthy of love. You're both worthy of so much love."

"I'm the one who's a monster," he whispers.

"You're human. Just like me. They broke us, but we survived." He swallows thickly, the muscles in his neck tightening. "We're not the same as we were, but we're healing, and that's what matters."

"You think you'll try to leave if I'm healed? Like if—"

"That's not going to happen." I lean up and kiss his lips. I mean these words with all my heart and all my soul. "I promise. It's just like I told Dean. You deserve more than me. I love you *so* much. There's nothing you could ever do that would make me not love you. I'll protect you from everything and everyone. I promise."

He drinks in that promise, whispering some of the words to himself.

"Do you love me too?"

"I only survived because of how much I love you."

The truth is in his eyes, undeniable and forever. I'll never have to spend a day without him once all this is over. It's so close I can almost taste it.

All the people who hurt us, gone for good, and then the rest of our lives.

That future begins here and now.

We start it with a kiss.

About the Authors

Willow Winters

Thank you so much for reading my romances. I'm just a stay at home Mom and an avid reader turned Author and I couldn't be happier.

I hope you love my books as much as I do!

More by Willow Winters
www.willowwinterswrites.com/books

Amelia Wilde

USA today bestselling author of dangerous contemporary romance and loves it a little too much. She lives in Michigan with her husband and daughters. She spends most of her time typing furiously on an iPad and appreciating the natural splendor of her home state from where she likes it best: inside.

More by Amelia Wilde
www.awilderomance.com/

This is the Discreet Edition
so no-one knows what you are reading.

You can find each edition at

www.willowwinterswrites.com/books

www.ingramcontent.com/pod-product-compliance
Lightning Source LLC
Chambersburg PA
CBHW020038310726
48970CB00007B/2314